Praise for *Diary of a Mistress*

"Miasha cleverly builds up the suspense and throws in several unexpected twists. Her latest release is filled with intrigue and will keep you turning the pages. *Diary of a Mistress* will make you think twice about who you trust."

—Sheila M. Goss, e-Spire Entertainment editor
and author of *My Invisible Husband*

"Miasha has done it again. *Diary of a Mistress* is a sizzling novel full of unexpected twists and guaranteed to leave readers in shock, and gasping for air, as they excitedly turn each page."

—Karen E. Quinones Miller, author of *Satin Doll,
I'm Telling,* and *Satin Nights*

"*Diary of a Mistress* is an intense, captivating, and twisted love triangle. Miasha allows the usually silent mistress to raise her voice through the pages of her diary."

—Daaimah S. Poole, author of *Ex-Girl to the Next Girl,
What's Real,* and *Got a Man*

"Only Miasha can make it hard to choose between wanting to be the mistress or the wife."

—Brenda L. Thomas, author of *Threesome,
Fourplay,* and *The Velvet Rope*

Praise for *Secret Society*

"Scandalous and engrossing, this debut from Miasha . . . shows her to be a writer to watch."

—*Publishers Weekly*

"An absorbing tale."

—*Booklist*

"A sizzling and steamy novel . . . the storyline will hold reader's attention and entertain them in the process."

—*Booking Matters Magazine*

"Miasha enters the arena of urban literature full throttle and ready to swing . . . surely to become one of the most talked about novels of 2006."

—Mahogany Book Club, Albany, NY

"Miasha cooks up a delicious drama with all the ingredients of a bestseller—seduction, vindication, and lots of scandal."

—Brenda L. Thomas, author of *Threesome,*
Fourplay, and *The Velvet Rope*

"Miasha tells it like it is. Her writing style is gritty and gripping, and will keep you reading and wanting more."

—Karen E. Quinones Miller, author of *Ida B*

"Miasha writes with the fatal stroke of a butcher knife. This book is raw material. Squeamish readers beware. You want proof? Just read the first page."

—Omar Tyree, *New York Times* bestseller and NAACP Image Award–winning author of the Flyy Girl trilogy, also known as The Urban Griot

"With *Secret Society,* readers should be prepared to expect the unexpected. Each page is a roller coaster ride of emotion, drama, and intrigue. Miasha packs her debut novel with so many scandalous scenarios that the reader can't help but anxiously turn the page in anticipation. An excellent debut that still has me shaking my head in amazement, long after I read the last page!"

—Tracy Brown, bestselling author of *Dime Piece,*
Black, and *Criminal Minded*

"Miasha writes with fire in this tale of two girls with a shocking secret and a story told with raw, heartfelt drama that is sure to carve this first-time novelist a place in the urban lit world."

—Crystal Lacey Winslow, bestselling author of *Life, Love & Loneliness*

"Miasha's careful composition brags a fast-moving plot with the twists and turns showing up at just the right moment. She constructed the characters quite well, as I became extremely connected with Celess and Tina, and each page was a deeper look into their hearts, minds, and essences. This story made me gasp, made me shake my head, and brought forth a level of insight I never thought possible."

—Rawsistaz.com

Mommy's
Angel

MIASHA

A Touchstone Book
Published by Simon & Schuster
New York   London   Toronto   Sydney

TOUCHSTONE
Rockefeller Center
1230 Avenue of the Americas
New York, NY 10020

Designed by Lorie Pagnozzi
Title page photograph © Lynn Saville/Getty Images

Manufactured in the United States of America

ISBN-13: 978-0-7394-8501-9

To all mothers—God's gift to you
is your children, and your children are
an extension of yourself. Do right by God's gift.
Do right by your children. Do right
by your extended self.

R.I.P Curtis

Stop playin'! Wet my hair and see what I do!" I yelled. Jamal was supposed to be washing his mom's car but he kept pointing that damn water hose in my direction, trying to mess up my jump.

"Aww, shut up, Angel! You ain't goin' do shit!" Jamal said, pointing the water at me again.

"MOM!" I yelled across the street. "Tell Jamal to leave me alone 'fore I hurt 'im!"

"Jamal, don't make me come down off these steps," my mom said with a smile on her face. "You can mess with anybody you want, but when it come to my kids, I'll beat ya ass."

"I ain't doin' nothin', Ms. Carmina," Jamal lied. "Ya daughter just mad 'cause she can't jump. She tryna find somebody to blame."

"Oh, please! I can jump!" I shouted. "You keep squirtin' me with that water and . . ." Just then Jamal pointed the hose at me again and water got in my mouth. That was it. I spit the water out in disgust and ran toward Jamal. He dropped the hose and took off. When I caught up to him halfway down the block, I slapped the shit out of him.

"Ahh shit! You heavy-handed!"

"Ha! Ha!" I laughed as I turned to walk back up the street. "Now, spray me with that water again!" I threatened.

The next thing I knew, Jamal had come up behind me and tried to put me in a chicken wing. I went wild on him, making it hard for him to restrain me. All the while he was getting his feels. But it was cool because I liked Jamal. He was cute, so he got a pass.

It was a typical summer evening. The sun had just gone down so it wasn't too hot. I was outside playing double Dutch with my friends, Shannon, Kim, Kiana, and Marie. My little sister Naja was riding her bike up and down the sidewalk. My mom was sitting on the stoop, braiding my baby brother Kindle's hair as he sat in her lap. Some guys had stapled a crate to the light pole, and they were using the corner as a basketball court. The little kids two doors down were playing red light, green light. Everybody was out.

I ran back up the street to get my jump, and my mom wasn't on the stoop no more. My baby brother was in his playpen on the porch, and my mom was in the rope.

"I'm comin' in, Mom," I said as I positioned myself to jump in the rope, counting to three in my head.

"No. I'm takin' ya jump," my mom said. "They was goin' gyp you."

With that said, I didn't jump in. I stood on the side and waited for my mom to finish. I needed her to get far so I wouldn't have to get the ends. I hoped she beat Kim and Marie, especially since they tried to be slick and gyp me. My mom missed on her walksies.

"Safe!" I said with attitude, and I did the cabbage patch in Marie's face as she went to get the ends.

"You lucky ya mom can jump, 'cause you wouldn't have beat me," Marie said.

"Well, it don't matter, 'cause my mom got my back."

"That's right," my mom said as she started to walk back over to the stoop. "Y'all goin' try to skip my daughter's jump and make her get the ends."

My friends chuckled at my mom, as they always did when she acted what they called young. To me it was just my mom being my mom, but to them she was the cool mom. Marie and Shannon started to turn the rope. We was playing Challenge and the first person in gets to choose what moves everybody has to do, so I wasted no time getting in. I was jumping, doing all kinds of moves, showing off. I could feel Jamal's eyes on me while he sprayed down his mom's car. Ever so often I peeped over at him. He would blush and then act like he was going to turn that damn hose on me again.

Skuuuurt!

My older brother Curtis's black convertible Mustang came speeding around the corner. Right behind him was another car, and from that car gunshots were being fired. The loud pops made everybody scatter. I remember running on the pavement and dropping to the ground with my hands over my head. After like a hundred gunshots and a loud crash, it was all over. My brother's car was smashed up against two parked cars, and the car that had been chasing him had swerved around his and disappeared off the block.

"CURTIS!" my mom's voice pierced my ears.

My mom ran over to my brother's car. In a panic, she tugged on the driver's door. When she finally got it open, my brother's body fell out into the street. My mom dropped to her knees and cried out for help. I was still on the ground looking up at it all, and it didn't seem real to me. Naja was walking her bike over to my mom with tears streaming down her face and Kindle was standing in his playpen throwing a tantrum. The neighbors began to slowly come back out of their homes and off their porches from hiding. Soon there was a circle of people surrounding my mom and brother. His blood was being washed down the street by the running water from the hose Jamal had abandoned. I couldn't seem to get up off the ground. I was terrified.

The police and paramedics swarmed the block within minutes. They taped up the scene and put my brother in a body bag. My brother's best friend, Antione, who had been in the passenger seat, was being put onto a stretcher. He hadn't been shot, but he couldn't move his legs. The paramedics said they were broken.

Just as they were putting Antione in the back of the ambulance, my mom ran over to him and started screaming, "Antione, what happened?! What went wrong?!"

Antione didn't respond, but he had a look on his face I would never forget, him and my mom both. It was a look of sorrow indeed, but, sorrow and so much more.

❖

Allow me to introduce myself. My name is Angel Carmina Washington. I'm fifteen years old in the ninth grade. I was born to a young and naïve Carmina Washington and a dead-beat alcoholic Andre Burke back in '91. I currently live in Brooklyn, New York, with my mom, her boyfriend Marvin, my little sister Naja, and my little brother Kindle. My older brother, Curtis, was killed two years ago, which is when the saga began. My mom took my brother's death hard. I mean, he was her firstborn and not only that, Curtis treated her like a queen. He cherished my mom and did everything in his power to make her happy.

My mom had been through a lot, especially with men. Curtis's dad left her when she was pregnant. Me and Naja's dad drank too much and abused her. And Kindle's dad turned out to be married and threatened my mom that he would take Kindle from her in a custody battle if she ever brought drama to his home. My mom never called him again after that. She really thought he would try to take a child he was not supposed to have in the first place. She didn't know any better. But through all the men and the bullshit they put her through, my mom always had Curtis right there by her side, making her feel special and giving her the love she desperately wanted. Curtis knew my mom was unhappy. He knew she had bad luck with men. So he was determined to step up to the plate and be the man of our house. He wanted so bad to make my mom's life easier. He wanted to take away her pain.

I remember days he would come in the house with flowers or perfume for my mom just to cheer her up. She was always crying or sad. It was always something about her owing people money, bills piling up, and her life not being fair. My brother couldn't stand to see her stressed, especially over money or men. And even though he was young, he felt it was his duty to take care of us as the man of the house. He started working odd jobs like delivering papers or bagging groceries at the supermarket, and every dime he got he gave it to my mom for bills or food. He was constantly out trying to make money, especially after my mom's only friend died and her son, Antione, moved in with us. My mom loved Antione like a son, but I often heard her tell Curtis that he was one more mouth to feed that she couldn't afford. My brother told her that things would be okay. None of us knew what he had up his sleeve. But we all trusted in him. He had managed to keep our household in order since he was like twelve, so we had no reasons not to.

Then when he was like sixteen, Curtis found the way to make good on his word and take care of us. He started DJing parties in the neighborhood. He was good at it, and the word got out about Cutty, his DJ name. Then he had got a job at a club. He was doing so well. He started having a lot of money. My mom started smiling more and stressing less. Her bills and debts were being paid. We all noticed a change in her. She was happier and that made my brother hustle more. He loved making my mom happy and seeing us okay. Eventually he got into making beats. The summer he turned eighteen he got offered twenty-five thousand dollars for one beat he had made. I remember he came in the house yelling. He had told us the news and we all danced in the living room. My mom was smiling from ear to ear. She was so happy she started crying. My brother told her she could tell her boss she only wanted to work part time. And then he had promised that once he got signed to be an in-house producer she would be able to quit altogether. That was his dream—to make beats exclusively for a major record label.

The good times were at an all-time high at our house. My mom had her days where she would be sitting at the dining table crying. But for the most part she was happy. Then my mom met a guy. She started spending a lot of time with him. She told us she had fallen in love with him. Then the next thing we knew she was pregnant. She was so excited and so were we. We planned a surprise baby shower for her and everything. It was nice. The only thing was her boyfriend didn't show up. My mom was upset. She called him and he didn't answer. It was like he had disappeared. She had my brother Kindle two weeks after the shower and her boyfriend still was nowhere to be found. We felt bad for my mom because she really thought that she had finally found the one. She got home with Kindle and she was depressed. She cried a lot. Then she started spending a lot of money. I'm not sure on what, but my brother used to plead with her to stop spending so much money. One day my mom decided to look her boyfriend up in the phone book since he had not been answering the number he had given her. Surely he was listed. She called him. I was sitting right there when she did it. I was watching TV, but I had one ear to her conversation. That was the day he told her not to ever call him again. He told her he was married with a family and that if she ever called him again he would take Kindle from her. She damn near lost it when she hung up the phone. She cried for days on end.

I took care of Kindle most of the time after that. Me and Naja. My mom just couldn't do it. She was too upset. And Curtis tried everything to make her feel better. He gave my mom money and gifts. He took us out to eat all the time so that my mom wouldn't have to cook. He was doing the best he could. Then after about eight months, he told my mom that things were about to get better. He got up one day, three days before his twentieth birthday, and he got dressed. Him and Antione got fresh. They had to go sell a beat Curtis had made and then they had a meeting with a record label exec. Curtis told my mom that if everything went the way he planned at the meeting she would never have to work again. My mom cried when he left, and she told him that he was the best son a mother could have. She told him that she wished she could have been a better mom to him. He told her that she did what she could and he appreciated her for that. He kissed her on the cheek, and then he told us to wish him luck. We were all happy for him. Me and Naja walked him outside and we stood in the doorway and watched him get in his Mustang with Antione and pull off. We couldn't wait for him to get back home that day and tell us the good news. Me and Naja were dancing around the house talking about our brother was about to be rich and famous.

"Curt about to blow up!" Naja said, squatting down with her hand over her mouth, copying a phrase and movement from Martin Lawrence.

We both laughed. My mom eventually joined in with our silliness, and the three of us were parading around the house celebrating. Little did we know Curtis would never get his chance.

Home Sweet Home

H i, Mom," I said dryly as I walked in from school. My mom was sitting on the couch staring into the blank television screen. A lit cigarette was hanging on the side of an already filled ashtray on the wooden coffee table in front of her. She was damn near lifeless just like she had been since Curtis died. My brother's murder affected a lot of people in a lot of ways. Antione moved out. I hardly went outside anymore. The whole block deadened. People were scared to sit on their front porches, fearful of stray bullets. But nobody was more impacted than my mom. She was never the same. The doctors said that she had fell into a depression that some pills would be able to control, but apparently the pills made it worse. She got hooked on them, and when they ran out she turned to alcohol. Eventually when the liquor wasn't easing her pain, she turned to heroin, her current drug of choice. And on top of that she met a drug-addict-pervert, Marvin, who she called her old man. And for the past nine months, we've all been forced to live as a family, which was, as you can imagine, *hell*.

I went straight upstairs to do my usual check on my little brother Kindle. He was only two and a half, so he wasn't in school yet. And my mom couldn't afford day care so he stayed home all day with my mom and her boyfriend. For that reason, I made it my business to make sure he had breakfast before I left for school in the morning and I checked in on him and spent a little time with him immediately after I got home from school.

"Angel," Marvin said as he exited the bathroom. "I didn't hear you come in."

I ignored him and proceeded to enter my little brother's room.

"Kindle is sleep," Marvin informed me, stopping me in my tracks. "Come here, though. I want you to read something for me," Marvin said, reaching out for my hand.

"Can't you bring it out here?" I asked, trying to be loud enough for my mother to hear me.

Marvin gripped my wrist and gave me the look that meant I'd better do as he said or else, so I went. Once inside my mom's barely furnished room, Marvin forcefully threw me on top of a mattress that my mother and him called their bed. He closed the bedroom door, first placing a towel between the door's lock and its frame, to keep it shut. Afterward he dragged his skeletal frame over to me casually. He began to unfasten his pants as he stood looking down on me as if I were a juicy steak dinner. His eyes were glassy and only half-way open. Droplets of sweat began to gather at his temples. He started licking his lips slowly. I closed my eyes to avoid the sight of him. I wanted to cry, but it wouldn't do anything but make him happier—so I didn't. I just laid there on my back and prayed while he had his way with me once more.

✿

"Naja Chanel Washington, *where have you been?*" My mother's high-pitched voice woke me out of my sleep.

I turned over slowly and looked at the purple alarm clock that sat on the computer desk in my room. It was 9:25 at night and my little sister was just coming in from school.

"I was over Aunt Jackie's!" Naja replied, with much attitude.

"You's a damn lie!" my mother retorted. Then she provided evidence. "I called Jackie and she said she ain't seened you all day! Now, I'm gonna ask you one more time, *where have you been?*"

"None of your business," Naja mumbled as I heard her attempt to dart up the steps. Naja lost more and more respect for my mom by the day. The next thing I knew, I heard tumbling and screaming, and by the time I was able to force myself out of bed Naja came storming into our bedroom, holding her anger-stricken face in her tiny rough hands. Before I could say a word, Marvin appeared at our doorway. He stood silent at first and picked his teeth with a toothpick. Seeing Marvin, I closed my legs tight and rested my arms in my lap. I could still feel the burning sensation he had caused hours earlier and I didn't want to give him any thoughts about doing it again.

"That's what the hell you get, runnin' around with those boys, comin' in here this time of night. You need to be more like your sister and come straight home from school!" Marvin had the nerve to say.

Meanwhile my mom was yelling, "Come on, let's go," to Marvin, and my sister was lying in her twin bed across the room crying. All I could think at that moment was how much I hated home.

Somebody Has to Feed Us

Boom! *Boom! Boom!* The loud knock on my bedroom wall woke me up bright and early, as it did every weekday morning. Shortly after, the phone rang. I turned over in my bed and reached my hand down, grabbing the phone off the receiver. I knew to answer. I knew it was for me.

"Good morning," I said, clearing my throat.

"You up?" Jamal asked in an upbeat tone.

I could hear loud rap music in the background.

"I'm not going to school today," I told him.

"Why not?" Jamal asked.

"Because yesterday I got into a fight and the principal said if I get into one more altercation this year they goin' kick me out. And I know if I go to school today that girl is gonna say somethin' slick out her mouth and Ima have to hit 'er."

"That's bullshit. You just started that school. They can't kick you out already," Jamal said in a know-it-all kind of way.

"Jamal, eight fights already—I'm surprised I'm still in the school as it is," I shot back at him.

"Damn, I ain't know it been that many. You been holdin' out on me, huh? You do need to chill out then, before they do kick ya ass out," Jamal said.

"I know," I said. "That's why I'm not goin' today. I need time to calm down and clear my head."

"Well, let's get together then," Jamal suggested, making plans with my time.

"What time do you get off? I can meet you at your house."

"I get off at six, but call up to the job at like one and act like you my mom. Tell 'em I got a family emergency and you need me to come home. You got the number," Jamal instructed.

"Okay," I responded, going along.

"I'm 'bout to bounce up outta here. I love you, boo," he said.

"I love you, too," I replied.

"Bye." He hung up.

Jamal had been my boyfriend for the longest. We lived right next door to each other our whole lives. We started out as childhood playmates and then we became best friends, and as we grew up we started really feeling each other. He was the only one who fully understood my situation. After all, he'd been there from the beginning, before Curtis died and my mom got strung out. So in addition to liking me, he felt sorry for me and he always made it his business to look out for me. I could talk to him about anything—well, except for Marvin, but that was only to protect him. I knew if Jamal ever found out about what Marvin did to me he would have probably killed him without thinking twice, and I didn't want Jamal going to jail for me or anybody, especially not no damn Marvin, so that was one thing I kept to myself. But for real though, I loved Jamal to death. He wasn't like most guys. He really cared about me. He was always on my case about school, and basically he picked up where my mom left off.

Speaking of school, on my list of places I hated most school came second to home. And it wasn't because I was like most people and just didn't like school because to be real school was all right to me. I mean, I got good grades and never had problems with my classes. It was just that it was high school, which meant it was a fashion show. Everybody dressed fly, well, at least all the girls. They wore only name-brand clothes and jewelry and their hair and nails stayed done. So for somebody like me, whose mom was smokin', it was hard for me to compete with them. I hardly wore name-brand clothes and when I did it was the off-the-rack kind, the defected stuff that got sold for cheap in the secondhand stores. And all the nice clothes I had when my brother was alive and we had money were too small, so whenever I tried to wear any of them, I got laughed at. I was constantly fighting to defend myself. So, no, I was not a troublemaker, but I was damned if I let those girls, specifically, Marie and her squad, call me all kinds of names. That explained the fights.

After hanging up with Jamal, I laid in bed a little longer contemplating what I was going to do that day. Through my half-open eyes I watched my little sister get ready for school. Naja was a shorter version of me, except she was a shade lighter than my golden complexion and she had a pair of dimples that were the only telltale sign of her being twelve years old. Her hair was as curly and jet-black as mine and she was as thick and overdeveloped as me, too. She sat on the edge of her bed and began digging through a trash bag of dirty clothes. She pulled out a pair of dingy jeans, shook them, and placed them on her bed. She then retrieved a pair of socks from the same bag. I turned over in my bed and faced the wall. The pictures of Jamal that were taped to the chipping paint made me grin. I felt tingly as I imagined hearing Jamal's knock sound through that wall. Whenever I heard that knock I knew it was a new day and everything that had happened before then didn't matter. It was out of my head. It was the past.

"Angel," Naja said as she gently nudged me on my arm.

"What?" I asked as I turned toward my sister.

"You got fifty cents so I can get a bagel?" she asked.

"Didn't Mommy go food shopping?" I questioned.

"No," Naja said with twisted lips and attitude. "She got her money yesterday, but she gave her card to Aunt Jackie," Naja explained.

I knew what that meant. Aunt Jackie let somebody spend all the money on the card for half the amount and her and my mom used the cash to get high. This happened often, at least every other month. It was only a few times that my mom actually had willpower enough to use her money on food as it was for.

"Naja, pass me my jeans," I said as I motioned for her to give me the pair of jeans that were draped over the foot of my bed frame.

I dug in all of the pockets and gathered the loose change. It totaled eighty-five cents. I dumped it into Naja's palm.

"Here."

"Thanks," she said as she headed out of our room. "I'll pay you back," she added as she left, possibly headed for school.

I closed my eyes to keep from crying. I couldn't believe how bad our situation had gotten in just a couple years. It was crazy how one day we had everything and hardly any worries and the next we were barely able to eat.

I decided just then that I would look for a job that day. I was not about to spend a whole day in the house with my mom and Marvin anyway. I got up, took a stand-up bath, put on some clothes, and left out.

The air was brisk and the wind was blowing hard. For a minute I wanted to turn around and get back into my bed, but I had a plan and I didn't want to put it off until another day. Besides, it was almost winter, so every day was bound to be that cold or colder. My plan was to go to all of the fast-food restaurants and fill out applications. I had to get a job. It was the only way I would be able to take care of Naja and Kindle, even if I only made enough to buy food. I stopped in

Wendy's first, being as though that was my favorite place to eat. I would love to work at Wendy's just to get free Junior Bacon Cheeseburgers and Frosties all the time.

I walked in the door and it was just a few people inside eating. I went up to the counter and approached an older gentleman.

"Hi, are y'all hiring?" I asked him.

"Actually we are. Do you have working papers?"

I looked at him dumbfounded. I wasn't sure what to say because I didn't know what working papers were. He must have figured that much out, too, because he followed up with a second question.

"How old are you?"

"Fifteen," I said quickly, happy to be asked something I knew the answer to.

"Oh," he sighed. "You have to be sixteen to work here. Sorry. Come back and see us on your next birthday."

I thanked him and walked back out into the cold. At that point my stomach started growling. I guess smelling all that good food in Wendy's reminded me that I hadn't eaten yet. I walked across the busy street and tried my luck at Dunkin' Donuts. Like I thought, they gave me the same sixteen-with-working papers routine.

Having no luck with the chain stores, I decided to try a few of the neighborhood mom-and-pop stores to see if they needed help, but they all told me that business was too slow for them to hire any more workers, part time or otherwise. I was about ready to give up on looking for a job. It was cold, I was hungry, and everybody was turning me away. I was upset because I felt stuck. I looked around and saw people walking and talking, driving and working. Everybody was going about their business, not thinking about me. I was nobody's concern. Whether me and my sister and brother ate or not didn't matter to any of them. I was on my own. And that was the first time I had ever felt a survival instinct. It seemed like my mind went into a whole other mode. I followed my instinct and raced up Flatbush Avenue to South Oxford. I walked two blocks up and reached my last resort. I was hesitant about knocking on doors because I had forgotten which house Antione lived in. Lucky for me, while I was contemplating, a black Porsche SUV came speeding down South Oxford. The driver swiftly maneuvered the truck into a parking space and out jumped Antione.

The last time Antione and I saw each other was two years ago at my brother's funeral. And even though we lived a hop, skip, and a jump away from each other, somehow I never ran into him and he never ran into me.

"Ant Man?" I asked reluctantly.

The tall, skinny, brown-skinned guy squinted his eyes as he walked in my direction.

"Angel?" he asked back.

"Yeah," I said with a smile on my face.

"What's up?" he asked as he cheerfully gave me a bear hug. "Look at you all grown up." He cracked a boyish smile.

I gave him a slight laugh and said, "I know."

"So what's up? What you doin' around here?" Antione

asked. But before I could respond he said, "Let's get out of the cold first."

I followed behind Antione as he approached his brownstone and unlocked his door.

"The hawk is out that ma'fucka," he said as he led me inside of his two-story apartment.

"Sit down, warm up," Antione said as he put the bag he was carrying on the bar that separated his kitchen and dining room.

I took a seat on Antione's white leather sectional.

"You want something to eat or drink?" he asked as he took off his tan Carhartt jacket.

"No, I'm all right," I said, lying, as I looked around the apartment.

Antione proceeded to take a platter of breakfast food out of the bag. He opened the top and steam floated from the food. The turkey bacon, cheese eggs, grits, home fries, and toast looked so good, and my stomach was empty, so I told the truth.

"You know what, I am kinda hungry," I said with a childish smile. I was embarrassed for some reason. I shouldn't have been, because Antione was like family.

"Come over here and get some of this food then. Don't be actin' shy," he said, making me feel a little more comfortable.

"So what's up, Angel. How you been? How's your mom and everybody?" Antione quizzed as he scooped food from his platter onto a paper plate he had gotten from off the counter.

I chuckled. I felt so silly. I didn't know why I was acting so bashful around somebody I had knew my whole life.

"What's so funny?" he asked, giving me a fork.

I immediately took a forkful of scrambled eggs to my mouth. The taste of those eggs could have made me sing. I haven't had breakfast like that in a while. I was used to eating cereal. Or if I had some change left over from lunch money Jamal would give me I would get a bagel and a juice.

"Ant Man, I need a huge favor," I blurted out after swallowing my food.

Antione looked at me confused. "What's that?" he asked.

I put on that stupid smile again and said, "I need a job."

"A job? You came down here after all this time to ask me about a job? Man, I thought you was coming to visit," Antione said as he dunked his toast in his grits and put the whole piece in his mouth. "Anyway, you too young to be workin'. Ain't you like fourteen, fifteen? You don't need to be worryin' about no job right now. You should be focused on school," he said in between chewing the toast and grits.

"I *need* a job, Ant Man," I said, sipping the orange juice he had poured for me.

Knowing exactly what I was getting at, Antione looked at me and said, "I don't know anybody that hire fourteen and fifteen year olds."

"That's why it would be a favor," I said.

Antione put his eating on hold and took a napkin from the bag the food came out of. He wiped his mouth and said,

"Angel, you're like my little sister. I can't put you out there like that."

I understood Antione completely, hell, I didn't want to put *myself* out there like that, but my home situation was getting the best of me, and my choices were very limited—if there were any at all.

"Ant Man, listen, you don't know how hard it's been on me, Naja, and Kindle since Curt died. My mom is gettin' worse, and somebody has to feed us," I told him. "You know I wouldn't even be comin' at you about nothing like this if I didn't desperately need it," I added.

"Yeah, but Curt wouldn't want me to put you onto somethin' like that," Antione said.

"I know, but he damn sure wouldn't want me in the position I'm in," I said, keeping it real. Antione knew like I knew that my brother took good care of us. We weren't rich or anything, but when he had money we had money. We never went without food and we always had nice clothes. "Ant Man, I ain't goin' lie to you, we goin' through hell over there. My house might as well be a crack house. The same house you damn near grew up in. My mom and her dude be gettin' high in there day and night. And Kindle be around it all the time 'cause he ain't in school yet. It don't be no food half the time. And look at me. Look at my clothes. I'm tellin' you, Ant Man, this is a cry for help. I tried the fast-food thing but they said I had to be sixteen. I just don't know what else to do," I pled my case.

Antione stood up from the bar stool he once was comfortably positioned on eating his breakfast. He looked me over and sighed. "I really don't want to do this, but," he said as he pulled a Louis Vuitton wallet from the back pocket of his Sean John jeans. He began his lecture as he surfed through a handful of business cards. "Angel, it has to be temporary, you hear me. Don't get comfortable. Get in and get out. Use the money to get y'all on y'all feet and as soon as you turn sixteen next year, get a real job," he demanded as he pulled a card from the bunch.

"I got you, Ant Man. I promise," I said with a serious tone.

"And you better keep going to school, and don't let nobody, I mean nobody, know what you do. Oh," he continued, "you better not get Naja involved. She's not as quick as you. She wouldn't last three seconds."

Antione handed me a black business card with silver lettering.

"Here," Antione said. "My man is the owner. Call him up and tell him that you're my little sister and I said it's cool for you to work there. He'll set you up from there."

"Thank you so much, Ant Man," I said, meaning it.

"Whatever, just remember what I told you," he said, getting back to his food.

We finished eating and I got ready to go. As I was leaving, Antione gently grabbed my arm.

"Ay, if you have any problems, any at all, come holla at me," he said with a serious face. "You know where I stay. Don't be no stranger."

I gave Antione my word that I would be all right and I left.

I had about two more hours before I was to call and get Jamal out of work so I decided to kill time at C & S's, the bodega around the corner from my house.

"Stay-cey," I sang as I walked into the cozy corner store.

"Hey, girlfriend, what's up?" Stacey asked with a slight Jamaican accent. "No school today?" she asked.

"Not for me," I replied.

"Girlfriend, what did I tell you about cutting school?" she asked jokingly.

Stacey was an old head, like thirty-one, but she was real cool. I looked up to her. She was kind of like a mentor to me. She was the only other person I could spill my guts to. Whenever I wanted to get out of the house I would just go to her store, well, her fiancé's store. She would hook me up with free sodas and chips and we would just sit and talk for hours until Cat, her fiancé, would come in and cuss us out for eating up everything without paying. He was all about money. He didn't even like his own girl to take free stuff. But I guess that was the way he had to be in order to make a profit and stay in business.

"Stacey, let me use the phone," I said.

"Girlfriend, you better hurry up before Cat comes back," she said as she took two quarters out of the cash register and slid them across the counter to me. I took the money and went to the back of the store where the telephone booth was.

I reached in my pocket and pulled out the business card I got from Antione. I put the fifty cents in the phone and dialed the numbers off the card.

"Hello, may I speak with Shake?" I asked in my most sophisticated voice.

"Who is this?" the husky voice on the other end of the phone asked.

"This is Angel. You don't know me, but my brother Antione told me to call you about getting some work."

"Antione, hahn? Well, how old are you?" he asked.

"Old enough," I answered, trying to sound mature.

"Old enough, hahn? Well, that's all I need to hear. Can you meet me at my club this Saturday?"

"Sure."

"All right. Let's make it like ten," he said.

"A.M. or P.M.?" I asked.

"P.M.," he confirmed.

Shake sounded impressed at how I handled our brief conversation and after giving me the directions to his club we hung up. Just as I put the phone on the hook, Cat came strolling in.

"*Bumblaclot!*" he yelled immediately. "What did I tell you 'bout making calls on me?" His heavy Jamaican accent bounced off the walls.

"Baby, chill out. It's only two quarters," Stacey said as she walked up to her man and caressed his chest.

He kissed her on her forehead, and although she was being sweet, he still had to make his point. "Quarters make dollars, Stacey," he said.

I just smiled. I was used to Cat fussing. I walked back to the front of the store and leaned against the counter. In admiration, I watched Cat and Stacey kiss each other on the lips. They were the cutest couple. Stacey was light brown like honey with hazel eyes and naturally straight hair that flowed down her back. You could tell she was Caribbean. Cat, on the other hand, looked like he was Hispanic, even though he had more Jamaican in him than Stacey did. He was light-skinned with thick wavy hair that he kept cut low. He had defined features, a pointy nose, Chinese eyes, full lips, and high cheekbones. The two of them were bound to make beautiful babies.

I interrupted their affectionate behavior and said, "Don't worry, Cat, in about a week, I'm goin' to pay you for every soda, bag of chips, and phone call I ever made, I promise."

Cat lifted his eyes off Stacey and directed them to me. "Is tat right?" he asked.

"Yeah, and matter fact, I'm going to add interest."

"You pullin' my leg, mon?"

"No. I'm dead serious," I said, smiling.

"All right," Cat said, "but if you don't make good on your promise, your ass will be out tere sweeping the front of this store every Saturday for a month, mon."

"No problem," I said with confidence.

I was feeling extra good about the possibility of getting a gig.

Ain't No Turning Back

The three days it took for Saturday to come seemed more like three months. I woke up that day as if it were Christmas morning. I wasn't able to sleep the night before. I was anxious about meeting Shake. So anxious, I got up at six forty-five and started cleaning the house. I even trashed my mom and Marvin's needles that I swore I'd never touch. By the time I had finished cleaning, I was hungry, but our last box of cereal had roaches in it, so I skipped breakfast and got dressed. Then I went in the basement and started rummaging through trash bags of summer clothes. I was looking for something I could take with me to Shake's just in case he wanted me to start working right away. I wanted to be prepared. I pulled out a bikini that I had since seventh grade. I washed it in the kitchen sink, wrang it out, and went upstairs to hang it on the radiator in my room to dry.

When I walked in my room I noticed Naja wasn't in her bed, which was unusual for ten o'clock on a Saturday morning. The bathroom was empty so she couldn't have been in there, and I had just come from downstairs so I knew she wasn't down there. I walked into my brother's room, and he was sound asleep. The only other option was my mom's room. The door was closed and the towel was in it. That meant "do not disturb," but I wanted to know where my sister was. I crept up to the door and tapped on it. No one responded.

"Mom," I called out.

"Whaaat?" my mom whined.

"I'm sorry to wake you up, but do you know where Naja is?" I asked nicely.

"Whaaat?" my mom whined again.

Then the door opened and Marvin appeared. He was buckling his belt, and with a frown on his face he said, "She'll be out in a second. Now go 'head back to doin' what you was doin'."

Past Marvin's skinny body I could see my mom sitting on the floor. Her back was leaning against her dresser. Her head was down as if she was sleeping. She had on a nightgown and there was a belt dangling from her arm. She had just shot up. And she was so high she could care less that her boyfriend was having sex with her twelve-year-old daughter right there in her bed. I couldn't see my sister, but I was determined to get her out of there.

"*Naja!*" I yelled. "*Come on! Get out of there!*"

Marvin intervened, "I said she'll be out in a minute. She's reading something for me. Now go on."

I was mad. I had taken all I could from Marvin at that point. It was one thing for him to get away with raping me, but I was not about to just stand around and let him take my little sister through that shit. He must have lost his mind. And the audacity to do it in front of my mom. Both of them done crossed the line.

"She ain't readin' nothin' for you. I ain't stupid," I yelled as tears gathered in my eyes.

Marvin ignored me and attempted to shut the door in my face. I pushed it open, hitting him in the process. He snapped' and back-slapped me. I lost my balance and fell on my butt.' The door shut and the towel was back in its position. I got up off the floor and ran down the steps. It was cold and I ran out of my house barefoot without a coat. I climbed the banister and started banging on Jamal's door.

"Yo, what happened?" Jamal asked as he opened his door.

I was so upset I couldn't talk. I just kept wiping my bloody nose with my pajama sleeve. Tears were pouring down my cheeks as I walked in Jamal's house.

Jamal comforted me. He sat me on his couch and held me in his arms.

"Whenever you get ready to talk I'll be ready to listen," he said, rubbing my head.

I wanted to tell him what had been going on in my house so bad, but I knew he would have went over there and hurt Marvin and then he would be the one going to jail. So I just sucked it up and decided to lie.

"Me and Naja got into it," I said.

Jamal smacked his teeth and said, "Y'all need to cut it out.

Y'all sisters. Y'all shouldn't even be fightin' like that, to the point that your nose is bleedin'. That ain't cool."

"I ain't wanna hurt her. That's the only reason why my nose is bleeding. If I would have fought her like she was a girl in the street I would have killed that little girl. That's why I just ran over here. I ain't wanna hurt her."

Jamal squeezed me in his arms. "You did right," he said as he wiped my tears.

I stayed over Jamal's that whole day. His mom was in Atlantic City, thank God, because I was not in the mood for her attitude. She was the one person who hated the fact that I was her son's girlfriend. And it wasn't about me being fifteen and him being eighteen. I think she felt like Jamal was too good for a junkie's daughter. She was one of them uppity ladies who thought her shit didn't stink.

We ate fish stick sandwiches and watched a movie on Showtime. Then we played Mortal Kombat on his PlayStation. And of course we did it. I loved doing it to Jamal. It was the only time I actually felt loved, safe, and happy. He was my first sexual partner. And if anyone deserved that title it was him. He respected me and he proved he wasn't after just one thing like Stacey warned of older guys. He really had love for me.

And the thing I loved most about Jamal was that he knew how his mom felt about me but he never once denied me or fronted on me. When it came to me, he would tell his mom to relax in a minute.

The sun had gone down and it was close to eight o'clock

by the time I woke up from a catnap. I sat up in Jamal's sofa bed and almost panicked. I looked around the basement and Jamal was on the other side playing Madden on the PlayStation.

"Why you let me sleep so late?" I asked him.

"You was chillin'," he said, not taking his eyes off the game.

"I told you I had orientation tonight," I said sweetly.

"I know. I was about to wake you up," he responded, his eyes still glued to the TV screen.

I put on my sweatpants and started to put on my pajama shirt, but I noticed the dried-up blood on the sleeve.

"Jamal, you got a old T-shirt I can put on?"

Jamal told me where his T-shirts were. I took one out of the bottom drawer and put it on inside out and all. I found my socks balled up underneath the sofa bed and started to put them on. Oh shit, I have to polish my toenails, I thought. I made up Jamal's bed and walked over to him to give him a kiss. He finally paused the game.

"I don't want you to go," he said kissing me on my lips.

"I don't wanna go, either, but I have to. My cousin put a good word in, and I don't want to make him look bad. I'm not even supposed to be working under sixteen," I explained.

Jamal walked me upstairs to the front door. We kissed each other again and I climbed the banister and went in my house.

I felt a little guilty that I had lied to Jamal about where I was going. I told him my cousin hooked me up with a housekeeping job at a hotel. But I couldn't tell him the truth. He would not have been able to handle it, even though he knew how desperate my situation was.

It was pitch dark in my house and cold. I clicked on the lamp by the door and walked over to turn on the heat. I went upstairs and looked in all the rooms. No one was home. I wondered where Naja and Kindle were. I was a little concerned. I hoped they were okay, especially Naja. I wondered if that was the first time Marvin had done that to her or had it been going on all along like with me.

I went in my room and turned on the light. I cut on the radio to listen to the countdown while I got dressed. I turned the volume up loud enough to hear it in the bathroom. It was still cold in the house so I ran the hot water and closed the bathroom door to warm the bathroom up. I took a quick bath and brushed my teeth. I borrowed Naja's Wet Seal jeans. I liked how her jeans fit my butt. I put on a white fitted shirt that had *baby phat* printed in silver across the chest. I slipped on my Air Force 1s, put on the Rocawear coat that my mom, Naja, and me shared, and headed out. I was carrying my book bag on my back. In it was the bikini I found earlier, a jar of Vaseline, and a bottle of perfume I got from off my mom's dresser.

Walking to the bus stop, I was shivering. I wasn't sure if it was because I was cold or nervous. It could have been both. I didn't know what to expect from meeting with Shake. *I mean, he sounded nice on the phone, but what if he was this big fat-ass arrogant nigga just out to take advantage of girls? Or what if he looked at me and said if you don't take your little young ass home? What if I see somebody in there that I know?* All types of thoughts were running through my head.

The 52 bus was right on time. I took it to the subway and took the subway over to Harlem. I got to Shake's fifteen minutes earlier than our ten o'clock agreement. The club was livelier than what I had thought it would be. Maybe I watched too much TV, because I imagined it being this small hole-in-the-wall bar with like two women dancing on poles and like six old drunk men watching them. But before I even got in the club, I could tell Shake's was nothing like I had imagined. There were cars double parked outside for blocks and they were hot cars, too, like Benzes and Lexuses. I grew more nervous as I approached the entrance.

I got inside Shake's and didn't know where to turn. It was packed. The air was misty and clogged with weed smoke. The lights were dimmed and the music thumped. I felt overwhelmed. My mind wasn't able to keep up with my eyes, and I couldn't hear myself think. I took a few deep breaths and tried to pull it together. I watched people pass by me and was ready to approach just anybody to ask about Shake, but I saw a waitress in the distance and decided to ask her instead.

"Hi, I'm Angel. I'm here to meet Shake," I said.

The tall, thick, light-skinned waitress frowned up her face and yelled over the music, "What? Speak up. I can't hear you."

"I'M HERE TO MEET SHAKE!" I raised my voice.

"Shake stepped out for a minute. Are you here for business or pleasure?"

"BUSINESS," I responded.

"Oh, well, follow me," she said, as she darted through the crowd carrying a tray of drinks.

I followed her to a table of straight dykes. I know, right—straight dykes? Anyway, the waitress placed the drinks on the table and turned to walk away when one of the butch-looking dykes smacked the shit out of her on her butt. I just knew the waitress chick was going to turn around and sucker punch the dyke, but she didn't. She just kept walking as if nothing happened. She led me over to a two-person booth in a smaller private room in the club.

"I'm Butter," the waitress finally introduced herself.

"I'm Angel," I said.

"So, what business do you have with Shake?" she said hurriedly.

"He told me to come down about working," I said, wondering where was Shake and why I couldn't talk to him.

"Well, Angel, how old are you? Because don't get me wrong, your body says twenty-five, but your face says twelve," Butter said, looking me up and down.

Trying to sound polite and stern at the same time, I answered, "Shake and I already discussed that."

Butter raised her eyebrows and began to give me the rundown. "Oh. Well," she, said smacking her teeth, "the dressing room is over there, right through those red doors. Go in there and change into your getup. When you're ready, meet me at the bar." Then she left out the room.

I walked out the room behind Butter. On my way to the red doors, I eyed the club. Chicks were dancing topless on the stage, doing nothing I hadn't already seen in movies. But on the floor, it was going down. Only porn movies exposed the kind of stuff the girls were doing down there. They were giving guys lap dances without their panties on and some of the guys actually had their things out. You do the math. Seeing that made chills creep up my spine. I wasn't sure I belonged there. But I didn't want to turn back, so I proceeded through the red doors.

There were about seven girls in the dressing room. One was counting money. Some were putting on makeup and changing. And a couple were just sitting down drinking water.

"Oh, girl, you ain't sayin' nothin', mommy! His dick was harder than that fuckin' math test I took last week!" a Hispanic-looking girl shouted.

"*Ahh ha!*" the other girls laughed as they slapped each other's hands.

The laughter and conversation came to a stop when I walked in. All the girls looked me up and down before any of them said a word.

"Look at this baby. She know she don't need to be in here," the Hispanic-looking girl said, as if I wasn't in the room.

The other girls just mumbled things under their breath and kept doing whatever they were doing. I was scared. I didn't know if I should have been a bitch and get in fight mode or been nice and broke the awkwardness.

I frowned up my face and got into defense mode. I was used to that option. Besides, I figured I couldn't show any weakness if I had planned to work there. I had to remember what I was there for and stick to my plan. It was like school—I didn't let Marie and them keep me from doing what I had to do there, and I wasn't about to let those old bitches keep me from doing what I had to do at Shake's.

I walked over to an empty station. I took off my coat and clothes. I wished it was a bathroom or somewhere private I could have changed, but it wasn't. I put on the bikini and God, my C cups were bustin' out of the extra-small top. More mumbles and some laughter resulted from me trying to squeeze my developed body into the bikini. I pretended like it didn't bother me, even though I was ready to cry.

Just as I was putting my clothes in my book bag, Butter walked in the dressing room with a husky brown-skinned guy. He was in his mid to late thirties and he dressed like it was the early nineties, in a Fila sweatsuit and Reeboks. He had on a lot of expensive-looking jewelry though. Butter and the guy walked over to me. The other girls played like they were busy but I saw them peeking over at me as the guy extended his hand to me.

"This is Shake," Butter said, introducing him.

I shook his hand and said, "It's nice to meet you."

He must have sensed my fear and discomfort because he said, "Don't be nervous. Angel, is it?"

I cracked a smile and nodded my head yes.

"See that, you're a gift from God," he said.

Butter cut in, "You want her to start now?"

"Hell yeah. They goin' go crazy for her. Those big-ass

titties and that pretty young face. Tell the DJ he goin' have to do a introduction for this one," Shake said as he practically fucked me with his eyes. "You're in good hands, baby girl. Butter'll take care of you," he continued as he turned to walk out the dressing room.

Butter rolled her eyes and said, "You ready?"

I felt so violated, but I held back my tears. "I think so," I said.

"Come on."

Butter took me over to the bar. She yelled out, "A solution drink," to the bartender, whose long micro-braids were the only thing covering her nipples. I sat down on the bar stool and peered around the club. Butterflies were having a party in my stomach. I was nervous as hell about getting up on that stage and dancing in front of a bunch of strangers. I didn't even know how I would dance.

"Here. Drink this. It'll calm your nerves," Butter said as she handed me a shot glass filled with brown liquid.

I gulped the alcohol down. It was disgusting. I almost choked. "Oh, my goodness, Butter, what the hell was that?" I asked, unable to keep from frowning.

Butter rolled her eyes for like the tenth time since I'd met her that night and said, "Don't ask questions you don't want the answers to." Then she slapped my leg and walked away.

"Here you go," the bartender said, sliding me a napkin. "Butter is a trip. But she don't mean no harm. Just try to stay on her good side and you'll be cool," she added.

I wiped my mouth with the napkin and grinned at the

bartender's advice. I chatted with her for just enough time to learn that her name was Fiesta and she had been bartending at Shake's for four months. After that the butterflies were gone and I was up on stage going buck wild. I was winding and twirling and even touching myself. I felt so turned on and so horny. It was like I had turned into a whole other person. It was strange, but it felt good. I had not a care in the world for those moments, and I drove the crowd crazy.

"Well, well, well," Shake said to me in the dressing room.

It was the end of the night, somewhere around four in the morning. I was putting back on my clothes.

"Somebody ain't no amateur," he continued.

"I don't know what got in me," I said innocently.

Then one of the other girls in the dressing room mumbled, "That E."

"Well, whatever it was. I hope it stay up in you. They was lovin' you, baby girl," Shake said, seemingly trying to cover up the girl's comment.

I wanted to ask the girl to repeat what she had said. But I was feeling dizzy and somewhat incoherent, so I let it ride. I just sat in the chair and tied my sneakers. Then I leaned my head back and called myself resting my eyes. The next thing I knew I was in the back of a cab and this strange foreign voice was yelling, "You're here, Ms."

I opened my eyes, which felt like they weighed a ton, and looked up at the cab driver.

"How much I owe you?" I asked.

"The guy took care of it already."

"Okay," I said, not knowing or caring what guy he was referring to.

I got out the cab and slowly walked up my steps and in my house holding on to the railing and the walls. I laid down on my bed and slept like I had been given anesthesia.

❄

"Angel, Angel!" Naja was calling my name.

"What?!" I jumped out my sleep.

"Where you get all this money from?" Naja asked. From what I could see she was holding two handfuls of ones and fives.

"Naja, what you doin' in my stuff?" I asked, not knowing how to justify the money. I looked down at myself and noticed I was still in my clothes and coat. My book bag was on my bed in the place of my pillow.

"It was all on the floor. It must have fell out ya pocket," Naja explained.

I took the money from her and came up with a lie. "I was gambling with Stacey and them at the store last night."

Naja ate it up. "For real. Oooh. Let me go with you next time. I'm tryna come up, too."

"I'll see," I said as I put the money in my book bag. I sat up in the bed and started to take my clothes off. It was ten o'clock in the morning, but I was still tired. I had every intention of putting on some pajamas and going back to sleep.

"Is they my jeans?" Naja asked as she watched me undress.

"Yeah. I borrowed them," I said.

"You goin' stretch 'em out of shape," she whined.

"Girl, please. Ya butt is 'bout as big as mine."

"Whatever. You owe me a pair of jeans. Shoot, with all that money you can buy me some new ones today."

That reminded me, I hadn't counted the money yet. After I changed my clothes, I took the money out of the book bag.

"Five, ten, fifteen, twenty, twenty-five, thirty, thirty-one, thirty-two, thirty-three, thirty-four, fifty-four, seventy-four, seventy-nine, eighty, eighty-one, eighty-two, eighty-three, eighty-eight," I counted.

"Oooh. You won eighty somethin'? Oooh, Angel, can I have some money? Can you buy me some sneaks? Can you get us some Boston Market tonight? Oooh, can we go shoppin'?" Naja asked.

"Pipe down," I said to my little sister. She sounded so money hungry, it made me worry. I didn't want her to end up doin' what I was doin' for a quick buck. Then the incident with Marvin popped in my head. I looked at my sister. She looked so innocent with her dimples and her baby hair. I couldn't imagine how she felt in that room like that. I had to ask her.

"Naja," I started.

"What? I can have some money?"

I sucked my teeth and said, "No, stupid. I wanna talk."

"About what? You goin' take us to Boston Market?"

"Naja! I'm bein' serious," I stressed.

"What?"

"What did Marvin do to you?"

Naja looked away and rolled her eyes up in her head.

"What are you talkin' about?"

"Yesterday morning. Did he do it to you?" I asked reluctantly.

"No! Is you crazy? I would have cut his thing off! Ill!"

"Well what did he have you in there doin'?"

"Nothin'."

"Naja, don't lie."

Her eyes went in her head again, and that time she didn't say anything.

"Naja, tell the truth."

"He tried," she said with an attitude.

My heart sank. I knew it, but didn't want it to be true. Tears formed in my eyes.

"And what happened?" I asked.

"He couldn't get it in." Naja went into tears.

I got up from my bed and went to hers. I put my arms around my sister and told her, "We're gonna have to put Boston Market on hold. I'm saving this money to get us out of this hellhole."

Home for the Holidays

It had been two weeks since I started at Shake's and it hadn't been half bad. It had actually been working out okay. Between the solution drinks Fiesta made me every time before I performed and the money that was waving in the air, stripping became bearable.

I managed to save six hundred dollars. That was after I bought food for the house and a couple new outfits for work. I even bought Naja some sneakers and a pair of jeans. I didn't know that stripping would be that profitable. I just expected to eat decent meals, but I was happy I was able to do more because I was determined to get a place for me, Naja, and Kindle. Even if I had to rent out a room somewhere, just as long as we were out of Marvin's reach.

My mom and I were on the bus on our way home from the

welfare office. She had to straighten some things out with her Access card and wanted me to go with her. Thanksgiving was days away and I could taste the food. But I knew my mom hadn't planned to cook because she wouldn't have any more money until the first of December. So I decided to make her a deal.

"Mom, if I buy the food, can you cook for Thanksgiving?" I asked.

"I don't care, Angel. But do you know how much a turkey goin' cost? Then you got the stuffin' and the macaroni and the candy yams. Then dessert, like banana pudding and sweet potato pie. That shit is expensive," my mom broke it down.

"I know. But I been saving some money. I want us to sit down and have a family dinner like we used to." I was excited just thinking about it.

My mom gave me a nasty look and said, "You sure been poppin' up with a lot of money lately. Let me find out you doin' somethin' you ain't got no business."

"Please. Like what?" I challenged my mom.

"Any fuckin' thing you ain't got no business doin'," my mom challenged me back.

"I told you already I got a job at a hotel."

"Yeah, well, all I know is it bet not get around, 'cause I heard they cut ya stamps off if they find out you got other money comin' in the house."

"Naw, it's under the table," I explained to my mom.

My mom reached up to pull on the wire that alerts the bus

driver to stop. We got off and started walking toward our house. When we got to the corner my mom stopped.

"Oh, wait. I gotta go past Jackie's house. Walk me around the corner," she said.

My mom and I walked side by side around the corner to Stuyvesant Street. When we got to Aunt Jackie's I sat on the sofa that was on her porch while we waited for somebody to answer the door.

"Heyyy," Aunt Jackie sang as she hugged my mom.

I was next. "Hey, Angel," she said, hugging me and kissing me and leaving a lipstick stain on my cheek.

"Hi, Aunt Jackie," I said, unenthused.

I didn't like Aunt Jackie. Then again, I didn't like any of the friends my mom made when she started getting high, and Aunt Jackie was one of them. My mom and her met through one of Aunt Jackie's sons. He was my mom's dealer.

"Ya daughter downstairs," Aunt Jackie told my mom.

"Who, Naja?" my mom asked, sitting down on the futon in Aunt Jackie's living room.

"Sit down, Angel," Aunt Jackie said as she sipped her Colt 45.

I moved some covers and a pillow to the side and sat next to my mom. Aunt Jackie sat in a wicker chair across from us.

"Yeah, she came over here straight from school, talkin' 'bout she was bored. I told her to go on down there and play that game with Kareem and them."

My mom rolled her eyes and said, "She don't need to be down there with them grown boys. She already fresh as it is."

"Oh, please. Shit, the girl said she was bored, so I told her to come in. What should I done, told her to go back home and sit up under Marvin and Kindle?" Aunt Jackie, said sipping her beer. "I'm glad I got four boys, geez."

"Jackie, shut ya drunk ass up and give me a cigarette," my mom said.

I got tired of sitting up there listening to my mom and Aunt Jackie talk trash to each other.

"I'm goin' downstairs with Naja," I said.

"Go 'head," Aunt Jackie said. "Give ya mom a heart attack. Both of her girls down there with my boys. Oh, Lord, y'all tryna kill the old lady."

I went in the basement, and Naja jumped up off Aunt Jackie's oldest son Kareem's lap.

"Angel, what you doin' here?" she asked, surprised.

I frowned up my face and said, "I should be askin' you that."

Naja positioned herself on the arm of the chair she was just sharing with Kareem, and they both picked up the Xbox joysticks as if they were playing all along.

"What's up, Angel, my buddy," Kareem said, trying to make light of the fact that his twenty-two-year-old self had my twelve-year-old sister on his lap.

"Don't what's-up-Angel me," I said as I sat down in a chair. "Where everybody at? Ya mom made it seem like y'all was down here playing the game." I picked up a *Source* magazine off the floor.

"Nasir and Sherif up at PAL and Hasaan over his baby mom house," Kareem told me.

"What, they up there playin' basketball?" I asked of Aunt Jackie's two younger sons, Nasir and Sherif.

"Yeah."

"Naja, you should've went with them. You need to be around guys ya own age," I said to my sister, still upset that she was down there on that old nigga's lap.

Naja sucked her teeth and smiled. "Shut up, Angel."

"Ain't no shut up, Angel. What if Mommy would have came down here and saw that. You know she would have drawed."

"Oh, please, she don't care." Naja rolled her eyes.

Before I could continue to drill Naja, my mom called me from upstairs.

"Give me that money for the turkey and stuff. Aunt Jackie goin' run me to the market," my mom said.

"What about me and Naja?"

"Y'all stay here 'til I get back."

I pulled my money from my jeans pocket. I counted out fifty dollars and gave it to my mom. I put the other twenty back in my pocket.

"That should be enough, right?" I asked.

"Yeah. We be back," my mom said.

After my mom left with Aunt Jackie I went back in the basement. I sat down there with Naja and Kareem for a while. Hours had went by since my mom had left to go to the market. I wanted to stay there and keep an eye on my sister, but I was getting bored.

"How can y'all sit here and play this game all day?"

"If you wanna leave you can leave," Naja said.

"I'm tryin' to wait for Mommy to come back."

"Her and my mom runnin' the streets. They ain't comin back no time soon," Kareem said.

"Won't you go around Jamal's house," Naja suggested.

I thought about it. I would have liked to be with my baby.

"Kareem, pass me the phone." I dialed Jamal's number.

"Hello," he answered on the first ring.

"What you doin'?" I asked, putting on my soft and sexy voice.

"Chillin'. Watchin' this TGIF shit," he said. "Where you at?"

"I'm around the corner. I'm 'bout to come over ya house."

"My mom just left for work, too," Jamal said.

"Oh, what, she workin' the night shift?"

"Yeah."

"Oh, that's what's up. Ima walk around there."

"Which way you comin'? From Ms. Jackie house or the store?"

"My Aunt Jackie house," I answered.

"All right. I'll meet you at the corner."

"All right. Bye."

I picked up my coat off the back of the chair and told Naja and Kareem I would holler. I didn't really want to leave Naja there by herself with Kareem. But I had rather her be with him than that damn Marvin.

It was almost dark outside. The streets were empty, with the exception of a few fiends scattered about and one or two hustlers on the Chinese store steps. By the time I got halfway up the block Jamal was on the corner standing there shivering his ass off. He didn't have on a coat or boots. Just some jeans, a white T, and some shower shoes with socks.

"Boy, you crazy comin' out the house like that. I know you is freezin' ya balls off," I told him when I reached the corner.

"I rushed out. I ain't want you walkin' around here by yaself," he said with his teeth chattering.

"All, ain't you sweet," I said as I wrapped my arm around his skinny waist.

Jamal's house was nice and toasty. It was like the heat gave me a big hug as soon as I walked through the door. He took my coat and we went in his room in the basement.

"This was right on time," he said as he hung my coat in his closet. "I was wondering when you was goin' call or come over."

"I was with my mom all day, takin' care of business," I said as I sat down on the sofa bed.

"I don't get that much time with you since you got that job. I ain't used to not hearing from you for days at a time," Jamal said as he sat beside me and started kissing my neck.

"I know. I know. I miss you, too," I said, closing my eyes. I was enjoying the feel of his lips on me. My whole body was enjoying his slightest touch.

He started unbuttoning my shirt and caressing my breasts with his hands. Then he started using his tongue on my nipples, bringing them to attention. I opened my legs, anticipating he would touch me there, and he did. I started moaning as I rubbed his body parts. We both reached for each other's pants button at the same time. Jamal laid me on my back and pulled my jeans off. He pulled my panties down and took one of my legs out, leaving the other in. He propped my legs up on his shoulders and started licking my private. It felt so good. I moaned and begged him not to stop. He got me so wet I could have flooded his basement. Then he slid his erect penis inside me. He laid on top of me, pumping and thrusting. After about twenty minutes we were both catching our breath on our way to sleep.

✽

Jamal's alarm clock was supposed to go off at six thirty but it didn't. Instead his mother woke us up when she got in from working overnight.

"Jamal!" the hefty, light-skinned woman shouted.

Jamal and I both jumped up.

"What the hell is going on here? This ain't no shelter. Um, excuse me, but you have to get out of my house. Jamal is not allowed to have certain people spend the night," she said nastily.

"Mom, chill," Jamal moaned.

"Chill? Boy, you must be kiddin' me. Until you start paying some bills around here you ain't allowed to say the word *chill*. Your ass'll be real chill outside in that cold. Now keep runnin' ya mouth," Jamal's mom said as she walked back up the basement stairs. "Should have took ya ass to college instead of chasin' behind some little fast-ass girl," she mumbled before she closed the basement door.

I sucked my teeth and started putting my clothes on.

"Little fast-ass girl," I repeated Jamal's mom under my breath. "She don't even know me like that."

Jamal put his arm around me and said, "Don't let that bother you. She just sayin' that to get you mad. You know how she is."

"This is all we needed. I thought you set your alarm."

"I did," Jamal said, reaching over me to get his clock. "I don't know what happened," he added, looking at the clock, trying to figure out what went wrong.

I got dressed and Jamal walked me to the door. Just as he was closing the door behind me I heard his mom yell from upstairs.

"A girl is as good as her mother. Remember that when you pickin' ya girlfriends!"

I had about enough of that lady's mouth. I wanted to kick her damn door down. But I just climbed the banister and went in my house.

"Hey, Kenny," I said to my little brother.

He was sitting on the couch watching cartoons.

"What you eatin'?" I asked him as I sat beside him.

"Cereal," he said holding a sandwich bag of Froot Loops up to my face.

"Umm," I said, "Can I have some?"

He nodded his head and gave me a handful of the dry cereal. I dumped them in my mouth. *Umm,* I thought, *I want some cereal.* I walked in the kitchen and got out a bowl and a spoon. I took the box of Froot Loops down off the top of the refrigerator and filled the bowl. I went in the refrigerator to get the milk and noticed that besides a half gallon of milk and a carton of orange juice the refrigerator was empty. I didn't see any eggs or shredded cheese for the macaroni and no onions or celery for the stuffing and gravy. I closed the refrigerator and opened the freezer. No turkey.

"Mom!" I shouted as I left out the kitchen and jogged up the steps. "Mom!"

My mom and Marvin were asleep on their mattress when I went in their room.

"Mom!" I called out.

"What, Angel?" my mom answered me, squinting her eyes.

"Where is the Thanksgiving food I gave you the money for?"

"Oh. Aunt Jackie goin' take me to the market later on," she said.

"Well, where is the money?"

"I got the money."

"Where is it?"

"Angel, talk to me about it when I get up, now," she whined.

I huffed and walked out my mom's room. I was so mad. She spent that fifty dollars I gave her. Her and Aunt Jackie probably went and got high. Talkin' about they was goin' to the market. I went in my room and Naja was asleep in her bed. I got my book bag out of the closet and took fifty dollars out of the six hundred. I was determined to have a Thanksgiving dinner, if not for me, for my sister and brother and even for my mom. I figured her sitting down and having dinner with us would remind her how our family used to be, and maybe that would make her want to get help. I didn't know. But I was willing to try. I wanted so bad to get things back to normal.

I ate my cereal, which I couldn't even enjoy, I was so mad. Then I washed up and threw on some clothes. I banged on the wall in my room to get Jamal's attention. He called my phone shortly after.

"What's up, boo?" he asked as soon as I said hello.

"Can you walk me to the market?"

"When? Now?"

"Yeah. My mom didn't get the food."

I guessed the crack in my voice let him know that I was hurt. He told me to give him a half hour and he would meet me outside.

Jamal and me walked up our street and turned the corner. Cat and Stacey were opening their store.

"You comin' around here to sweep up?" Cat asked as he saw me approaching.

I chuckled.

"Cat, leave Angel alone," Stacey said, unlocking the door to go inside the store.

"What's up man?" Jamal spoke and shook Cat's hand. "Hey, how you doin'?" he greeted Stacey, too.

Stacey and Cat gestured for us to come in the store. We followed their lead.

"Where y'all goin' dis early on a Saturday?" Stacey asked, taking off her full length fur coat.

"She was on her way 'round here to sweep outside, I told you," Cat said.

It was a good thing I had brought extra money out the house because that was the perfect opportunity to make good on my promise to Cat. I pulled out a twenty-dollar bill and put it in Cat's hand.

"Now you sweep the front of ya own store," I teased.

"Ohhh," he said. "She played me."

Stacey and Jamal laughed.

"Tats wassup, mon. You are now officially my favorite customer," Cat said.

He walked behind the counter and opened the register. He put the twenty in it and took out a five and a ten.

"Here, mon. Your change," he said, handing me the money.

I shook my head no.

"Girl, you better take that money," Stacey said.

"No. It's cool. Y'all looked out a lot," I said, heading for the door. "I'll be back around. I'm about to go to the market," I told Stacey as I left the store.

Jamal wasted no time asking me what the transaction between me and Cat was about.

"You know how Stacey always be giving me free stuff? Well, Cat be cursin' us out about it. So when I found out I got the job, I told him I would pay him back, and he was like if not I gotta sweep outside the store every Saturday," I explained.

"Well, you should have took that change," Jamal said. "I

understand you got a job now, but you can't be too generous with ya money."

"It's not like I can't make it back," I told him, subconsciously thinking about the night I had ahead of me and the tips I was bound to make.

"You talk like it's sweet at your job. I might have to go with you tonight and fill out a app."

"They don't take applications at night," I told him.

"Well, bring me one home. I'll take it up there Monday morning," he said.

I didn't want to make up another excuse about the issue and make him suspicious, so I just agreed to bring him an application.

Me and Jamal spent more time in the market than we needed to. We debated about almost every item I wanted to put in the cart. *Why you gettin' jumbo eggs, get large. That kind of cheese don't melt right. What you goin' do with celery? Ain't you supposed to use bread crumbs in stuffin'?*

By the time I got back home and put the food away, it was lunchtime and I was hungry. I made me and Naja a Ellio's Pizza. I was surprised she was home. Since that day Marvin did what he did, she been getting dressed and leaving out as soon as she woke up.

"Umm, how you get the crust so crispy?" Naja asked as she took a bite out her pizza. "My crust always be soft."

"Put it directly on the rack," I told her, pouring juice in our cups.

I sat at the kitchen table with my sister. Kindle was still in the living room watching TV.

"Thank you," Naja came out and said.

"For what?" I asked, taking a piece of my pizza to my mouth.

"For buying us food and stuff. Our 'frigerator ain't been full in a while," Naja explained.

"Y'all my family. That's what I'm supposed to do," I told Naja.

"Yeah, but you could spend ya money on yaself and like buy us stuff off the dollar menu at McDonald's."

"You give a man fish, he'll eat for a day. You teach 'im how to fish, he'll eat for good."

"What's that supposed to mean?"

I broke it down for my sister, "I could buy y'all a dollar this and a dollar that. But that only lasts a day. But if I go to the market and keep our kitchen stocked, y'all will have food every day. The bottom line is, whoever is able to feed us should, and that person should show us how to feed ourselves so if that person ever becomes unable to feed us then we'll be all right on our own. So don't thank me, learn from me. And God forbid anything ever happens to me, you'll be able to do this for yourself and Kenny."

Naja nodded her head as if to say she understood. I loved my little sister and grew more emotional every time it dawned on me that she was virtually my responsibility. I figured I had to teach her as much as I could so that she could be responsible on her own. God knew my mom wasn't in the position to show her, so it was up to me. And I was ready for the challenge. I was serious about getting us out of my mom's house, and at the rate I had been going at Shake's my goal could be achieved by the new year. That mental reminder amped me up for work that night.

❋

I got to work at nine thirty. The girls that hated on me my first night had become my friends. Whenever I walked into the dressing room they smiled at me and spoke. I figured it was because of how much Shake favored me. They either was scared that I would rat them out if they gave me any problems and risk losing their job or maybe they were using me to get closer to the boss. I wasn't sure, but I was sure of one thing, they weren't no real friends.

"Hey, Angel!" the three girls that were in the dressing room greeted me.

"Hey, Chestnut. What's up, Sugar. Hey, Baby Doll," I spoke back.

At my station I started to change. The girls got back to their conversations about the tips they were making, their customers' preferences, and sex stories whether with their partners or clients.

In a short while Butter walked through the door with a guy I had seen in the club once or twice. My natural reaction was to grab hold of my titties to keep him from seeing my nipples.

"Yeah right, like he ain't seen 'em before," Butter commented on my instinctual act.

"I know, right," Chestnut agreed in laughter.

I felt a little embarrassed that I had been the only one covering up in front of the guy. The other girls carried on as usual, one of them butt naked.

My mind worked fast and I said, "Yeah, but not without paying."

Butter did what she was known for and rolled her eyes. Nobody said anything back. They just snickered at me. The guy even chuckled. Then he followed Butter to her station, one away from mine. Out the corner of my eye, I watched him give Butter some blue pills. She gave him some money, and he walked out of the dressing room alone. Butter then sat in her chair and grabbed the spring water bottle that was filled with something much darker than water and opened the cap. She put one of the pills in her mouth and followed up with a swallow of the unknown drink. She put the rest of the pills in a Motrin bottle that she took out her makeup bag and then went back onto the floor.

"What you lookin' at?" Chestnut asked.

I guessed she had noticed me watching Butter.

"Nothin'. What you talkin' about?"

"You was all up in Butter mouth," she continued.

"What? You ain't never seen nobody pop a E-pill before?" Sugar butted in.

"I don't know what y'all talkin' about. What Butter do is Butter's business," I said.

"She probably wanted one for herself," Baby Doll suggested. "She be on 'em all the time."

"I know that's right," Chestnut and Sugar cosigned.

"What is y'all talkin' about?" I asked, frustrated.

Chestnut pulled one of Butter's numbers and rolled her eyes. "Tell me you don't be poppin' E every time before you go on stage."

"She do. She go right up to Fiesta and sip it down with that Hen," Sugar concluded.

"Sugar, I take a shot of liquor, yeah, but I don't fuck with no E-pills, damn."

"Ohhhh," Baby Doll sang as if she had learned a secret. "They do what they did to that other chick, what's her name?" Baby Doll started snapping her fingers.

"The Puerto Rican girl?" Sugar asked.

"Yeah, what's her name?" Baby Doll asked.

"Ria," Sugar answered.

"Yeah, that's it. Remember when she first started here they put the pill in her drink and she got sick?"

"That's right. They sure did," Chestnut jumped back in.

"Whatever happened to her?" Baby Doll asked.

"I heard she strung out," Sugar said.

"Yeah. I heard that, too," Chestnut added.

"So y'all sayin' Fiesta be puttin' E in my drinks?" I snapped.

"Basically," Chestnut said. "I know what a bitch on E look like, and you be that bitch every time you up in this muthafucka."

I said no more. I finished getting changed and left the dressing room. I wanted to find out if what they had told me was true. I didn't know much about E-pills. I mean, I heard rappers say stuff about them in songs, but that was it.

"Fiesta!" I yelled over the music.

Fiesta turned around to face me. She put a finger up and told me she would be over to me in a minute. She fixed a drink and put it in front of a customer, picked up her tip, and walked over to me.

"What's up. You ready for ya solution drink?" she asked picking up the bottle that stored the Hennessy.

"No, no. I gotta ask you something."

"Oh, what's up?"

"Do you got any E-pills?" I leaned over and asked her in her ear. I didn't want to come right out and ask had she been putting pills in my so-called solution drinks because if she sensed my anger she would have probably lied.

"Of course. You want one?" she responded proudly.

"Do what you do," I told her, still feeling her out.

She winked her eye at me and poured the Hennessy in a shot glass. She then put the glass under the counter, and that time I actually paid attention to what she was doing. She had dropped a tiny blue pill in my drink at the same time that she put an ice cube in it. She gave me the drink and smiled.

"You been doin' this all this time?" I asked her.

She frowned her face up and said, "Yeah."

"I didn't know that," I said, innocently enough.

"You didn't? Well, I thought you did. I mean, Butter did come over here and ask for a solution drink right in front of your face."

"That was my first night here. I thought that was just the name of the damn drink," I told her.

"Well, sorry. I won't put none in ya drinks no more," she said casually, as if it were no big deal.

"It's cool. You ain't know," I told her. I wasn't mad at Fiesta. Butter was to blame. But I didn't trip. I figured it was nothing to worry about since everybody seemed to be cool about it and I wasn't sick or anything. I just felt some type of way when Chestnut and them told me shit was being put in my drink without me knowing. I don't play that shit. Too many people get strung out after shit like that, and one of my biggest fears was becoming a fiend. After seeing how crazy that shit got my mom, I vowed that would never be me.

I sat down on the bar stool and looked around the club. I was feeling funny, like depressed. I didn't feel like working. I wanted to take a shot like I usually did to get me in my zone, but I doubted it would work the same without the pill in it. And I didn't want to request the pill because then I would have felt like I had become dependent upon it. I didn't know what to do. I just sat there watching the other girls work—some on the stage dancing and others giving lap dances. I watched them closely. They all seemed to have the same glare in their eyes and the same passion in their performances. I couldn't help but guess that they were all on E. All that time I had thought it was just alcohol. Silly me. I had gotten myself in some shit I wasn't sure I knew how to get out of.

"Either pull some money out and start tippin' a bitch or get ya ass up on that stage and do ya job. It's too packed in here for you to be wastin' space." Butter approached me from out of nowhere.

"Butter, I don't feel good," I told her.

"Well, get you a drink and feel better," she commanded. "Do somethin' other than sit there and pout."

Butter went behind the bar and picked up a tray of drinks. She shot a quick glance at me and then went back into the crowd. Fiesta must have heard what Butter told me because she slid me a drink.

"It's straight," Fiesta answered my question before I could ask it. "It should help you loosen up at the least."

I picked up the shot glass and hesitantly took it back. I frowned up my face and let out a deep breath. I waited for the Hennessy to kick in, and all that happened was I felt buzzed. I felt like telling jokes and laughing. Now, that might have worked if I had been going on stage at a comedy show, but it didn't help me get naked. And I needed something that would. All the other girls were up there getting paid while I was sitting at the bar getting drunk.

"You want another one?" Fiesta asked me.

"Make it a solution," I said, desperate for the reaction I had got used to getting. I figured if it wasn't broke I wasn't going to try to fix it. I had done all right that far. And besides, I had only been getting them three days a week at work. It wasn't like I was poppin' pills on the regular. And if it helped me make money, then it would have to do, because that's what I was there for in the first place. The conversation I had earlier with Naja played in my head, and I took the solution drink back without a second thought.

I started feeling the effects of the pill and was back in the groove of things. Before long I was on stage doing my thing, clapping my butt cheeks, caressing my breasts, and opening my legs in guys' faces. They loved it. The tips started to pour in and I was glad I hadn't let the news of me taking E-pills get the best of me because I would have left the club that night without a dime.

When I was done with my dance, I went and sat at the bar. That time it was just to get some water. This guy came over and sat beside me. He was a young guy, like in his early twenties. He had on some jeans, a hoodie, and some Tims. I looked him over briefly but I didn't say anything to him. I just sipped on my water.

"I liked what you did up there. You dance good," the guy said to me after he shouted his order to Fiesta.

"Thank you," I said, smiling, still under the influence.

"How about you give me a private dance?" he asked.

"A private dance, huh? Well, I never did one before."

"It's a first time for everything," he responded, looking at my body.

Just his voice alone turned me on, and the way he looked at me, like he desired me, made me so wet.

"Plus, it's worth a lot more than a stage dance," he added, rubbing a hundred dollar bill over my breasts.

Oh, God, that felt so good, I thought. I led him to the small room in the club that Butter took me to for our initial meeting. I could have done it right there at one of the tables, but I didn't want the whole club to see me give my first lap dance. Inside the small room there were only six chairs. One girl was in there with a guy. The other five chairs were empty. A bouncer stood by the entrance. I took my customer to the chair farthest away from the other girl. I wanted as much privacy as I could get. The guy sat down and put his hands on my hips. I stood in between his legs for a moment and guided his hands up and down my thighs. After feeling the music and getting hornier I sat down on his lap from behind and started grinding on him. He was squeezing my butt cheeks and I was loving it. His dick got hard so fast I wouldn't had been surprised if he had came in his jeans. I spent a few minutes in one position and then a few minutes from the front. He was rubbing my breasts and I put them in his face. I wanted him to put them in his mouth so bad. I was winding on him and we were touching each other. It was like we were having sex with our clothes on. Well, technically I was naked with the exception of a g-string. But he was fully clothed.

"I want you to suck my dick," the guy whispered in my ear.

I was in la-la land feeling overly sexual and was more than willing to honor his wishes at that time. I slid off his lap and onto my knees. I unzipped his jeans and pulled his penis out. Without thought I put my mouth on him.

I had made one hundred and fifty dollars off that one guy and I didn't even get his name. I liked it that way, though. That's what made it exciting. That was the first night I left Shake's feeling good about my job. And it wasn't just about the money that night, it was about the control. I started taking E-pills willingly from that night on. They made me be the person I needed to be while I was at work, and that increased my profit.

The Difference a Day Makes

Ring! The bell for lunch rang in the middle of my science teacher giving the class our homework assignment. I packed up my book bag and headed into the crowded hallway.

"Angel," a guy's voice called out.

I turned to see who was calling me, and it was Marie's boyfriend, Kevin. What the hell did he want? I wondered. He knew me and his girl didn't like each other. Why was he calling me?

"What's up?" I asked him.

"Come here for a minute. Let me holla at you real quick," Kevin said flirtatiously, posted up against his locker.

I laughed at him. He must have bumped his head. First of all, I had a boyfriend. Second, before I started dressing all right and getting my hair done he ain't have nothin' to say to me. Third, he was Marie's and I wanted nothing to do with anybody who had something to do with that bitch.

I started to tell him how I felt about his silly ass, but before I could speak a familiar voice shouted out.

"OH NO, BITCH!"

Just as I had turned around to correct Marie, her balled fist came right at my face. In a matter of minutes I was pulled off of Marie by a school security guard.

People lined the halls and watched me get dragged to the principal's office. The principal, Mrs. Keen, was furious when the guard told her that it was me who had been in a fight.

She called me over to her desk with an angry look. I walked over there feeling like I had lost before the battle even began. I knew I wasn't in the wrong for that fight. I simply defended myself. But the look on Mrs. Keen's face told me that she was not going to be trying to hear any of that.

"Angel, I warned you," were the first words that came out Mrs. Keen's mouth. "Now, this is unacceptable. Nine fights before the first marking period. There is absolutely no way I can excuse this."

I snapped, "She started with me!"

"I don't want to hear that! There are other ways to handle confrontations."

"Like what? What should I have done after she punched me in my face?" I asked, frustrated. I was sick of being the underdog. I was tired of being hated on, teased, laughed at, and then being blamed every time I fought back.

"You are not in any position to ask questions, young lady," Mrs. Keen said as she cut her eyes at me.

"Well, then don't ask me no questions either!"

"You know, Angel, you are going to be one of those people who make life harder than it has to be. I gave you chance after chance to redeem yourself. All of your teachers say that you are one of their best students. School could be a breeze for you, but . . ."

"Exactly," I jumped in. "Did you ever stop to ask yourself why I fight so much and why it's always the same girl? I'm tellin' you, she always startin' with me! She punched me in my fuckin' face! What I'm supposed to do after that?"

"First off, watch your mouth in my office! Second, there are going to be Maries everywhere you go. You need to learn how to deal with them appropriately, and beating on them is not the way. And you know what I find interesting? According to you she's always the aggressor, but yet she's the one who ends up with bruises and scars."

"It ain't my fault she can't fight!" I jumped in again.

Mrs. Keen gave me a look. She was upset. I guessed she wanted me to just sit there and shut up while she chewed me to pieces. She was out her damn mind.

"*Be quiet!*" she said sternly.

I rolled my eyes.

"Now, the last fight, her mother threatened to press charges against you and the school. I told her that if she didn't, I would personally see to it that her daughter would never have another altercation with you again. And look what happened. It wasn't enough for me to threaten to expel you? That didn't play in your head at all this afternoon did it?"

At that point I knew what it was. Mrs. Keen was under pressure to keep her promise to Marie's mom, so regardless whose fault it was or what I had to say, it didn't matter. The only thing that mattered was Marie's mom.

"Well, if this is about moms, then, yeah, I lost. My mom ain't comin' up here raisin' hell for me. Look at my face. I have a scratch on it, too, but my mom ain't threatenin' to press charges on nobody. And if that's what it takes to keep me from getting kicked out, then I have no win 'cause my mom ain't doin' it. So go 'head and expel me. Make Marie's mom happy! I could give a fuck!" I snapped.

I got up and left Mrs. Keen's office. When I walked out the doors of the school, I didn't look back. I was too through with those people. All they cared about was the school's reputation. They didn't give a damn about the students, and damn sure not me.

It was only one o'clock, and I wasn't ready to go home. I wished Jamal was home—I would have kicked it with him. But he was at work and didn't get off until that evening. I figured I would go chill with Stacey and tell her what happened. I needed to blow off some steam. It was warm outside for November and it showed. Newton's Laundromat was packed, everybody was out on Bedford Ave., and the Louis Armstrong Projects were hittin'. The kids were out jumping rope and runnin' around. The older people were sitting in their kitchen chairs in front of their doors. And of course the hustlers were out on every corner, occasionally making hand-to-hand sales, but for the most part playing ball with the little boys.

"Hey, Stacey," I said, as I walked in C & S's.

Stacey was behind the counter watching the stories. The store was empty. She hadn't got hit with the after-school traffic yet.

"Hey, girlfriend," Stacey said joyfully. "What you doin' out of school?"

I twisted up my lips and told her, "I got some bad news."

"What happened?" she asked as she walked from behind the counter and leaned up against the deep freezer. "You were in a fight?" She obviously noticed the scratch under my eye.

"Yeah. But before you lecture me about how not cute it is to be fightin', let me tell you the whole story."

"I'm listening," Stacey said.

"You know the girl Marie who . . ."

Stacey cut me off and said, "Oh, Lord, not her again."

"Yes. Anyway, her boyfriend tried to holla at me in the hallway and . . ."

"And you gave him the time of day?"

"No, no. Listen," I whined.

"Oh, my bad. Go 'head."

"So, I was about to tell him I was cool, and here she come out of nowhere calling me a B. Then she swung on me. I had to fight her after that," I recalled.

"Um, um, um. So, what, you got suspended?"

"Worse," I said, regretful.

"What?"

"They kicked me out."

Stacey's bottom lip dropped. "No they didn't."

"Stacey, I am so pissed off," I said.

"You should be. What are you goin' do? How are you goin' get ya education?"

"I don't know. Mrs. Keen made me so mad. I just walked out on her."

"Who's that, your teacher?"

"No. The principal."

"You walked out on your principal? Oh, girlfriend, you in hot water."

I took a deep breath. "I know."

"So, what you goin' do?"

"I don't know. If my mom had her act together I would have her go up there and curse everybody out. That's what Marie mom did and that's why I'm the one that got kicked out and she didn't. But . . ."

Cat walked in the store, interrupting me and Stacey.

"What it is, my favorite customer?" Cat greeted me loud and cheerful.

"Hey, Cat," I said with a slight smile.

"Hey, baby," Stacey said, hugging Cat.

"You goin' be doin' a lot more than hugging me when you see what Daddy got for you," Cat said, handing Stacey two plane tickets.

Stacey looked at the tickets and then jumped up and down like they were winning lottery tickets.

"Oh, my God, Cat, you got 'em! We're goin'? For real?" she shouted.

"Where y'all goin'?" I asked, trying to peek over at the tickets.

"Oh, girl," she began. "We're going to Jamaica."

"That's what's up," I said. "When are y'all goin'?"

"We're leaving Wednesday!" she said excitedly. "We haven't been back home in a while, and I told Cat I wish we could spend the holidays with our families."

"So y'all goin' down there for Thanksgiving?"

"Thanksgiving, Christmas, and the New Year," Cat informed me. "We won't be back in here until the day after New Year's."

Stacey screamed with happiness. "Oh, my God. I have so much packing to do!"

"What about the store?" I asked. "How y'all just goin close the store for that long?"

"My brother goin' run it for us," Cat said. "We need a break."

"But what am I goin' do for so long without y'all," I whined. Cat thought I was just joking, but Stacey knew I was serious. She knew that her store was like a safe haven for me.

"Girlfriend, you'll be all right. That time is gonna fly by so fast you not goin' know we left," she said. "And if you need me to I'll go up to your school when we get back." She winked her eye at me.

I appreciated the gesture but was still upset that they were leaving. I was happy for them just sad for me. I wished they could have took me with them. I would have loved to go to Jamaica—shit, I would have loved to go anywhere away from home.

I left C & S's right before the elementary kids rushed the store. When I got home Naja was in our room on the phone. Kindle was in there with her scribbling on a shoebox top.

"What's up, y'all," I said, sitting on my bed.

Naja waved and Kindle said hi, but both continued doing what they were doing.

"Where Mommy at?" I asked.

"In her room," Naja answered.

"Marvin in there, too?" I asked.

Naja shook her head.

"Hold on," she told whoever she was talking to. "Him and Mommy got in a fight and he left," she said, smiling.

"Did he hit 'er?" I asked, almost whispering. I didn't want Kindle to hear me.

"Yup," Naja said, going back to her phone conversation.

"He a sorry son of a bitch. He lucky Curt ain't alive. His ass would be . . ."

Naja nodded and said, "I hope he stay gone."

I took off my school uniform and threw on some chill clothes. I went downstairs to the kitchen to start dinner. I decided I would make spaghetti. It was the only other meal I knew how to cook besides chicken wings and boxed maca-roni. I started thinking about my older brother Curt and how much things would have been different had he been alive. He would have been twenty-four. He was a lot older than me, but we were close. I remember he used to pick me and Naja up from elementary school and take us shopping at the Manhattan Mall. Those were the days. I wished he were still with us so bad. He would have never saw us living like we did. My mom probably would have never got strung out in the first place. And Curt damn sure would not have had Marvin in this house.

I drained the ground beef and put the spaghetti in the boiling water. I stirred the sauce and poured the meat in it slowly. While I waited for the spaghetti to get done I set the kitchen table. Kindle came in the kitchen before I yelled for him and Naja to come eat. I guessed he was hungry.

"What you cookin'?" he asked me, standing on his toes trying to see on top of the stove.

"Step back. It's hot," I told him. "Matter fact, go upstairs and wash your hands and tell Naja to come on and eat."

"You made spaghetti?" My mom appeared in the kitchen.

"I thought you was sleep," I said, without looking at my mom.

"Put a plate up for me, okay? I'm goin' around Jackie's."

"You want to eat now with us?" I asked my mom, finally looking at her bruised face.

I hoped she would say yes, because then she wouldn't have went and got high. That would have been one less bag of dope being put in her system.

"No. I'm not hungry right now. I need to go around the corner. Aunt Jackie got some money for me," she said as she took our Rocawear coat off the basement door and put it on. She dug into the pockets and asked me, "Where my ciga-rettes at?"

"I don't know."

"They was in my pockets. Who wore this jacket last?"

"Naja," I told her.

"Naja!" my mom yelled upstairs.

"What?" Naja yelled back.

"You seen my cigarettes in my coat pocket?"

"It was only one in there," Naja yelled.

"Well, where is it?"

"I gave it to my friend!"

"What you mean, you gave it to ya friend! Keep ya fuckin' hands off my shit, okay! You ain't grown!"

My mom came back into the kitchen. She was upset.

"Angel, give me five dollars until I get back from Aunt Jackie's."

"Ain't you about to go get money from Aunt Jackie now?" I asked my mom, recalling her excuse for not having dinner with us.

"Yeah. But I wanna stop at C & S's and get some cigarettes first. I'll give it right back to you. That damn sister of yours giving my cigarettes away like she paid for 'em or somethin'."

I didn't feel like going back and forth with my mom. I was hungry and I had a bad day as it was, so I gave her five dollars so that she could go about her business.

Naja, Kindle, and me ate dinner at the table like a family. They complimented me on my good cooking. I put my mom up a plate and put the rest of the food in the refrigerator. I got Kindle out of the dirty pajamas he had on all day and realized he didn't have any more clean ones. I organized his dirty clothes into piles of darks and whites and put them in separate trash bags. I gathered me and Naja's dirty clothes, too, and made it my plan to go to the Laundromat that next day, especially since I couldn't go to school.

It was about ten o'clock when I started feeling aches in my body, probably from the fight I had. I laid down in my bed and was so tired I wound up falling asleep without calling Jamal at eleven like I had done every Monday night that he worked late.

I was in a good sleep when I heard rummaging in my room. I woke up, and through the dark I saw my mom going through my drawers like she was looking for something.

"Mom, what are you doin'? It's twelve o'clock at night. What are you looking for?" I asked her.

She ignored me, continuing to dig through my stuff like a frantic robber.

"Mom! Stop! What is wrong with you?"

"Where that money at? Where it's at?" my mom asked me, scratching and sniffing.

She was skitzin' and I didn't know what to do. That was the first time I had seen her like that. I tried to snap her out of it, but she was in her own world, fiending, determined to find my money and get a hit.

"What money? You don't have any money in here!" I told her.

By then Naja woke up.

"What's going on?" she asked.

I got up out my bed and turned on the light.

"Angel, just give me a couple dollars. Just give me like twenty dollars," she said. She was sweating and shivering.

I was scared. I never saw my mom like that. I didn't want

to give her any money, but she needed it so bad. She looked sick and she was acting crazy. I didn't know what she would do if I didn't give her some money.

I went to the closet and took my book bag out.

"Uhn-uhn. Don't give her no money," Naja advised me.

"*Naja! Shut up!*" my mom shouted.

I opened my book bag to take out a twenty and looked up at my sister to give her a look to be quiet. I didn't want them to get into it, especially while my mom was in that strange state of mind.

Suddenly my mom snatched the book bag and ran out my room. I chased her down the steps and grabbed her shirt, spinning her around to face me. She hauled off and punched me. I lost my balance and took a few steps back. I didn't know if it was shock or my mom's strength that had me feeling like I couldn't move.

Naja had my back. She charged at my mom and tried to get my book bag from her. They tugged on it all the way to the front door. Then Marvin showed up. He must have been on the porch the whole time. And I was sure he had put my mom up to stealing from me. He pried Naja's hands off the book bag and pushed my sister to the ground. Meanwhile my mom hurried off the porch.

I regained myself and ran to the door. Marvin stopped me in my tracks. He stood in front of me, holding me back by my neck. I started crying and screaming at the same time.

"I HATE YOU! I HATE YOU, MOM! HOW YOU GOIN' STEAL FROM ME, YOUR OWN DAUGHTER? HOW YOU GOIN' DO THIS TO ME?"

I whaled off and started swinging on Marvin. He let me go and ran off the porch. I dropped to the floor, still in the doorway of my house, halfway in and halfway out. I started sobbing uncontrollably. Naja hugged me and cried with me. She knew just as I knew that all the money I had saved was in that book bag—and with it in the hands of Marvin and my mom we were back at square one—stuck there, stuck in that house. I couldn't take it.

I jumped up and went upstairs to my room. I started putting clothes on top of my pajamas. I threw on my coat and sneakers and let my hair out of its wrap.

Naja was right behind me. "Where you goin'?" she asked, wiping her eyes.

"I be back. Stay here with Kindle," I told her.

"Where you goin'?" she whined.

"I'm goin' to Aunt Jackie's to get my fuckin' money before that bitch of a mother we got shoot it all up."

"Let me go with you. I wanna fuck her up for you," Naja said, still crying.

"No. Kindle can't be here by hisself. I'll be all right," I said as I left.

It was dark and it had gotten cold outside. I speed walked up the street and around the corner. A few smokers were scattered about in front of C&S's, probably waiting for their dealers. I spoke to the ones that I knew and kept on to Aunt Jackie's. My heart was racing. I wanted to really hurt my mom and Marvin.

Knock! Knock! Knock! Knock! Knock!
Knock! Knock! Knock! Knock! Knock!

I was banging on Aunt Jackie's door like I was the cops. I didn't care either. I wanted my money.

"What the hell?" Aunt Jackie answered the door. "Angel, what is wrong with you? Banging on my door like that this time of night. It better be a life-or-death situation, missy."

"Is my mom here?" I asked with an attitude.

"No, she ain't here, but come in and tell me what's going on."

"She ain't here? Did she come by here? Or did Marvin come by here?"

"No. Come in the house out of the cold and tell me what the problem is."

I walked in Aunt Jackie's house. "Is Haas here?"

"Hasaan ain't been here in days. Why? What the hell is going on with you?"

I started to tell Aunt Jackie what had happened, but that would have been a waste of time. She wouldn't have done nothing about it and plus I wanted to try to find my mom before it was too late. She couldn't have gone far. And if she didn't buy from Hasaan, then the only other person would have been the dealer on my block.

"I'll tell you later. I gotta go," I told Aunt Jackie and walked out her house.

"You don't need to be in the streets this late, Angel," Aunt Jackie yelled from her doorway. I was almost at the corner of her block, and I wasn't tryna hear that. I wanted my money back.

I walked back around to my block and knocked on the

crack house door. The fat guy who rented the house came to the door.

"What's up, Angel?" he asked casually, like it wasn't my first time knocking on his door. I mean, we spoke when we saw each other in the street, but I never knocked on his door before.

"What's up, Mr. Carl? Is my mom in there?"

"Naw," he said simply.

"All right," I said and walked off the porch.

It was getting windy and I was tired of looking for my mom. I was sure her and Marvin gave my money to a dope man by then anyway. The thought of that brought tears to my eyes. I felt myself getting angry all over again. I desperately needed to be with Jamal at that time. I didn't care that it was late. I was going to knock on his door. I needed him more than anything.

I walked up to his house and saw the light from the TV glowing through his basement window. I felt a sense of relief knowing that he was probably awake. I decided to knock on the basement window instead of the front door. After a few soft knocks, he appeared at the window. His face was frowned up. I thought it was because he was shocked that I was knocking on his window at that hour. But when he came to the door I was in for a rude awakening.

"What the fuck you want?" he asked me.

At first, I couldn't speak. I was so confused. My face was scrunched up.

"Jamal, this is not the time for nothing petty, and if you're actin' like this because I didn't call you at eleven o'clock then that definitely qualifies as petty," I told him, trying to be as calm as possible.

"You think I give a fuck that you ain't call me at eleven. I could care less if you never call me again," he said with an anger-stricken face.

"What the fuck?" I shouted. "I can't catch a break. First my mom and her bullshit and now this? What is it about?"

"Don't try to make me feel sorry for you, 'cause I don't. You act like ya life is so fucked up all the time when you come around me, but you all laughs and smiles when you suckin' a nigga dick at the strip club."

"Oh, my God, what are you talkin' about?" I remembered the episode that Jamal was talking about, but I had to deny it. I didn't mean to do that. I was high as hell. But I didn't think it would get back to him. And if it did he couldn't have had solid proof, so I just figured I'd deny it to the very end.

"Don't play stupid. My young bull showed me the pictures on his phone."

"What? What young bull? What pictures? What are you talking about?"

At that point I started getting scared. If that nigga snapped pictures of me with his camera phone then that was it. There was no way I could deny it. I was caught.

"He work at my fuckin' job, and he showed all of us in the break room you givin' him head in a club. I can't believe you. My mom was right about you. You lied to me this whole time about being a housekeeper at a hotel. You really been dancin' naked for a bunch of niggas and apparently suckin' all they dicks. I don't got no love for you no more, man. You did me dirty. I don't want nothin' to do with you. So take ya problems to them niggas." *Boom!*

Jamal said what he had to say and shut the door in my face. I couldn't even defend myself. He was right. I was wrong. Dead wrong. I should have never went that far in the club. Jamal been nothing but good to me, and I fucked up. I knew he was hurt. He had to be. He put a lot into me and took a lot from his mom for me and I stabbed him in his back. I was so mad at myself I could have slit my wrist right then and there if I had a blade. Seeing Jamal hurt like that made me feel worse than how I felt about what my mom just did. I thought I was going to lose my mind. I felt so much emotional pain. I needed something. But I didn't know what. I just knew that I couldn't go home. I was too hurt to go home and be reminded of what my mom did.

I walked the few blocks to Antione's house stumbling over my own feet, mumbling to myself, and fighting tears the whole way. I was messed up. Somebody could have snatched me up and ended my life and I wouldn't have cared. I rang Antione's bell. He answered the door and panicked.

"Angel? What happened? Who did this to you?" he asked, looking at my face, seemingly half asleep. I must have had a bruise or something from when my mom punched me. He let me in and I plopped down on his sofa.

"One of them niggas at the club? Which one? I will kill that pussy!" Antione went on as he wiped crust out his eyes.

I shook my head no and mumbled, "My mom."

Antione stopped ranting and raving about what he was

going to do to the nigga who hit me, and he sat down beside me. He had a serious but sincere look on his face. "Damn, Angel, she's that bad now?" he asked of my mother.

I nodded yes, and the tears poured out. I dropped my head in Antione's lap. Antione rubbed my head. It was obvious he didn't know what to say. But I guessed he felt so bad that he had to offer something.

"You want to smoke a blunt with me?" he asked.

"Please," I said in desperation. I had never smoked weed a day in my life before then, but I had heard that it made people's pain go away. And at that moment all I wanted was for my pain to go away.

Antione lifted my head off his lap and retrieved a bag of weed and a cigar from a box on his coffee table. I watched him empty the cigar and begin to fill it with the weed.

"Yo, what happened?" he asked as he rolled the blunt.

I shook my head and started to explain. "In one day, I got kicked out of school, my mom stole all the money I had saved up, and the only person I did have in my corner told me he don't want nothin' to do with me because he seen pictures of me dancin' in the club that he didn't even know I worked at. What the fuck did I do to deserve this day," I cried.

Antione didn't respond. He just shook his head. He seemed like he felt sorry for me and wanted to make me feel better as fast as he could because he started licking the blunt quickly. He lit it and gave it to me first. I didn't know what to do with it. I couldn't stop crying, and I had never smoked a blunt before. I put it in my mouth and inhaled. I started choking. Antione took the blunt out my hand and patted my back.

"You gotta take your time. And try to stop crying first," he instructed. He took a puff and I watched him.

I reached out for the blunt and gave it another try. I got it right that time, and after a short while I found what it was that I needed.

No Place Like Home

It was Thanksgiving Day. I woke up with a smile on my face. My mom was going to cook all that food I bought and we were going to have dinner like we used to. I couldn't wait. I sat up in the bed and looked across the room, but my sister's bed wasn't there. Oh, shit, I thought, I'm not home. I'm still at Antione's. My smile turned into a frown and my joy into sadness. All the shit that happened three days before came to mind. I started feeling mad again, especially since I had looked forward to spending the holiday with my family. I wanted to cry. But I didn't. I just got out the bed and went in the bathroom. I rolled a blunt with the weed me and Antione had left over from the night before. I lit it up and sat down on the toilet seat and smoked it.

When I got done I washed my hands and went downstairs. Antione wasn't there. I went in the kitchen to make a bowl of cereal. Antione's kitchen was spotless. It looked like he never cooked one day in there. His pots and pans looked brand new, and he had the good kind, too. They were stainless-steel nonstick. This was no place like home. All I needed was my sister and brother with me and I would have been cool. I made a mental note to call and check on Naja and Kindle when I finished eating. I hadn't spoken to them since I left. I hadn't done much of anything for that matter, except eat, sleep, and smoke weed. I needed that rest though. I had to get my mind together for work. I had to build my stash up from scratch again, so it was no time for me to be takin' my problems to work.

I poured the milk in my bowl of Cap'n Crunch and sat at the bar. I turned on the plasma TV Antione had on the wall in his living room and turned to the parade. I remember Curtis took us down to the Macy's parade one year. It was cold as shit. But we had fun, though. I missed my brother so much.

I got up to get an ice cube from the ice maker and heard keys in the front door. Antione walked in with a big alumi-num pan and like six other pans were on the doorstep.

"You need help?" I asked, walking toward him.

"Yeah, take this," he said, handing me the big pan.

"Ummm," I said, getting a whiff of the food. "What's all this?"

"It's our Thanksgiving grub," he responded, carrying in all of the other pans.

"For real?" I squealed. "This is what's up!"

I put the pan down on the counter and lifted the corner of the top to get a peek at what was in it.

"Macaroni and cheese!"

"Here," Antione said as he put another big pan down on the counter. "Put this one in the oven."

"What's in that?" I asked.

"I think it's the greens."

Antione put another pan on the counter as I put the pan of greens in the oven.

"Can this one fit in there too?" he asked, handing me another big pan.

I took the pan from him and smelled the top trying to figure out what it was. It smelled like yams. I hoped I was right. I put it on the bottom oven rack.

"Where you get all this food from?" I asked.

"Sylvia's," he said nonchalantly, as if Sylvia's didn't have the best soul food in New York.

"Sylvia's hooked you up!"

"Yeah, they always look out for me."

Antione and me put the rest of the pans wherever we could fit them. Some in the refrigerator, on the counter, and on the dining room table. It was food everywhere. I couldn't wait until dinnertime.

I watched the rest of the parade with Antione as we reminisced about Curtis. And all that reminiscing made me want to see Naja and Kindle, so I got dressed, wrapped up some of the food Antione had bought to take to my sister and brother, and walked to my mom's house. I needed to get some clothes anyway.

"Hi, Angel," Kindle took his eyes off the cartoons to speak to me when I walked in the door. My mom's house was a mess. Kindle's toys were scattered about the living room. Marvin's sneakers and clothes were thrown around. The coffee table was covered with mail and newspapers, and cigarette butts and ashes were sprinkled about as if someone dumped the ashtrays onto the floor.

"Hey, big boy. Come give me a hug," I told my brother as I cleared a spot on the table for the food I'd brought.

I sat on the couch and Kindle jumped into my arms. He needed a haircut and his nose was crusty like he had a cold.

"You sick?" I asked, holding him on my lap.

He nodded his head yes. I kissed him on his cheek and put him down. I went in the kitchen to put the food away and turn on the oven to heat the house up some. Dirty dishes were piled in the sink. Nothing was cooking. It was Thanksgiving, for God's sake.

"Where's Naja?" I asked Kindle, walking back into the living room.

"Upstairs, I think."

I went upstairs. My room door was closed. I went in. Naja was in the bed asleep. She must have been cold, because even with the kerosene heater on, she was snuggled up in my and her comforter and still in her clothes.

"Naja," I whispered, tapping my sister.

"Angel?" she asked, waking from her sleep. "Where you been at?"

"I had to get away from here," I told her, not answering her question. I didn't want Naja to know that I've been staying at Antione's because she would have wanted to stay there, too, and that wouldn't have worked for a few reasons. Number one, I didn't want to turn Antione's house into a shelter. Number two, I didn't want her to be in there with Antione alone on the days I would be at work. And number three, I wasn't sure how long I would be staying there myself, and I didn't want her to be moving all around with me.

"Why you leave me here?" Naja asked, frowning.

"I can't take you and Kindle with me just yet, but I will. I just need a little bit of time to get some more money saved up."

"You staying with Jamal, ain't you?" she guessed.

"Naw," I said. Damn, I wished I was though. I still hadn't gotten over our breakup. I called him every day that I've been gone and apologized on his answering machine, but he hadn't called me back. Naja was goin' make me want some weed, bringing up Jamal.

"Well, where you been? I know you wasn't at Aunt Jackie's 'cause I been over there," she continued.

"Don't worry about that. But you shouldn't be over Aunt Jackie's house like that. Kindle need somebody here with him to make sure he eat and stuff. And if you do go around there, take him with you."

"He be all right," Naja whined.

"Just do what I told you," I stressed.

"Well, are you staying here?" Naja asked, after rolling her eyes at my demand.

"No. I just came to see y'all and drop off some food and to get some clothes."

"You brought some food?" Naja asked, enthused.

"Yeah. From Sylvia's. It's enough for like a week."

Naja came from beneath the covers and jumped out of the bed. She wasted no time getting down to the kitchen. Sometimes I thought she was more greedy than hungry because she got way too excited over food.

"Hooo!" Naja sang as she danced around the food in the kitchen.

She took a plate out of the sink, rinsed it, and put it on the table. Then she got a fork out of one the drawers.

"I'm 'bout to throw down!"

Her loud mouth must have piqued Kindle's curiosity, because he came into the kitchen.

"What's that? Can I have some?"

I smiled to myself at the sight of my younger siblings. I was happy when they were happy. I took my coat off and decided to stay longer than my initial plans of a few minutes. I figured my mom and Marvin were in their room and not up in my face so I could bear being there for a while. Plus, I wanted to spend some more time with Naja and Kindle.

I washed a plate for Kindle and fixed his food. I washed the dishes while he and Naja ate.

"Um, um, um," Naja moaned as she chewed her food. "Angel, you a life saver."

"You cooked this food?" Kindle asked.

"No. I bought it. It's good?"

Kindle nodded. I believed him, too, because he was tearing that food up.

"You not goin' eat?" Naja asked.

"Yeah. Later."

"When? When you get back to your new house?" she asked with an attitude.

"It's not my new house. I told you I was coming back. Just not now," I explained myself.

I knew Naja felt some type of way that I was leaving and not telling her where I was going. I knew she really just wanted to go with me. I felt bad that she couldn't. Antione's house was so much nicer than here, and he had heat and food and no drama, shit, he was barely there. It was clean all the time and just peaceful. I wanted that kind of household for Naja and Kindle so bad. That was why I started working at Shake's in the first place. I felt obligated to take my brother Curt's place. Curtis made sure we lived well and I admired him for that, and since he wasn't there and I was the next oldest I had to step up to the plate. But who knew it would be this difficult? Who knew the roadblocks would come so frequently? I was almost there. I almost had enough for at least a security deposit somewhere. And my mom fucked it all up. I would never forgive her for that. She really messed my head up doin' that. It was no way I could stay in that house with her after that, even if I wanted to. I just had to go back to Shake's the next day and work like it was my first day all over again. I had to put in some overtime and try to get my stash back up quickly. I gave myself a month. There in the kitchen over the sink, I told myself that I had thirty days to save money, find a place, and move in it with Naja and Kindle.

"By Christmas, we all goin' be out of here," I told Naja.

"What's happenin' between now and then?" she asked.

"I'm getting us a place." I meant what I said with all my heart. I wanted that very thing badly, and I was willing to do whatever it took to get it.

❋

It had only been a week, but when I walked inside of Shake's I felt like a stranger. I felt weird and my nerves were uneasy. I took it as me being emotional about all the stuff that had happened over the course of a few days and ignored the bad vibes. I went into the dressing room and changed and then went over to the bar. I ordered a solution drink from Fiesta.

While waiting for the drink, I scanned the club. It wasn't as packed as it usually was on a Friday. I guessed the men were at home with their families being it was the day after the holiday. Fiesta handed me my drink and I took it with me as I walked the club. I made casual conversation with some of the other dancers, catching up on any gossip I may have missed and spoke to a few of the customers. When I finished my drink and began to feel the effects of the Ecstasy, I got up on stage and started working. Men immediately flocked to me, tipping me instantly. I closed my eyes and got into it, clearing my mind and letting myself go. I let the music control my every move, and the men loved it. I even noticed Shake eying me rather hard. When I returned the stare, I saw Butter get up from the seat next to him and storm away. I didn't care. I was feeling that shit. The attention was just what I needed. Plus, I had a mission, and Butter's attitude was not going to get in the way of it. My mind and my body were completely free.

Then, suddenly, out of nowhere, a group of policemen burst in the doors with their guns drawn.

"Freeze! Nobody move!" an officer yelled.

Every corner of Shake's filled with policemen. The few people that tried to run or hide was placed in handcuffs. One cop dressed in plainclothes flashed a piece of paper in front of Shake, who was one of the few in handcuffs. He said something about a warrant. The other cops were reading the detainees their rights. Some of the girls that I worked with were caught in the act of having sex, and they were immediately arrested. I was glad I hadn't started any of that yet. Pretty much the whole club was under arrest, with the exception of some customers and Butter. I looked around and didn't see her anywhere. And before long, I, too, had handcuffs on my wrists. The fact that I was high and told a cop that I was old enough when he asked my age, is what did it. I didn't learn that until I was at the police station and they told me I had been arrested for underage drinking.

In all my fifteen years of living I never thought I'd go to jail. But there I was. I was in a cell with some of the other girls I worked with, and they were all talking.

"I do not believe this shit!" one of them said.

"You? I'm supposed to work my second job in the morning," another one mentioned.

"What, at the Gap? You can miss a day at the Gap. It ain't like it's a real job," a third one gave her opinion.

"I called out today to work Shake's and they was pissed because it's Black Friday," the second one explained.

"You worried about the Gap. Girl please, I got three kids at home. How I'm s'posed to explain to them and the babysitter that I ain't comin' home tonight," the first one said.

I just sat there watching them go back and forth. I didn't have anything to complain about. I didn't have kids or another job to get to. My only concern was getting out. I never been locked up before. I didn't know the procedure or what to expect. For all I knew I would get some time. But then again, I did hear of people being let go when they were minors, so . . .

"Angel Washington," a policewoman called out as she opened the cell. I picked my head up and the officer nodded for me to follow her.

"Where she goin'?" somebody mumbled.

I followed the woman to a room, or rather a hallway.

"You need to call your mother or legal guardian. Because you are under eighteen, she can come down here and sign you out. You will just have to appear in court in about thirty days. There go the phone over there," she told me.

You would think I would have been relieved. But any bad situation that required my mom was one I could count on getting worse. My mom wasn't reliable, period. I picked up the phone anyway. I dialed my mom in hopes I was wrong this one time.

"Mom!" I damn near shouted when I heard her say hello.

"Angel?" my mom asked, sounding sleepy.

"Mom, I need you come down to the police station and get me." I didn't hesitate.

"Police station? You ain't been home in days and you call me asking me to come get you from a police station? What you done did anyway?"

I lowered my voice and tried to have patience with my mom, even though I was fed up with her. "Underage drinking. But I only had one drink at this club."

"See that. Welcome to the real world. I'm glad you got a dose of reality. You don't have nothing goin' for you. So get used to this kind of shit. You just like me, like how I was when I was your age. Some people are just chosen, and people like us just ain't," she told me.

I huffed and rolled my eyes. I wasn't tryna hear that shit. I didn't believe one word of it. I was nothing like my mom, and I was determined to keep it that way. I just went along with her because I needed her. Otherwise I would have hung up on her.

"Can you come down here? I don't have all day on the phone."

"How I'ma get there? I don't get no money to the first."

"Just get money from somebody, and I'll give it back."

"Who goin' give me some money?"

"You only need carfare. Like five dollars. You can get five dollars from Marvin."

"Marvin ain't got no money. He just gave me his last twenty to go to the Laundromat earlier."

I was getting frustrated. My mom was actin' like it was

impossible for her to gather five dollars to come get me out of jail, but let her need a hit, she would find a way to get that money.

"All right. Well if I have somebody pick you up and bring you, you goin' come?" I thought about Antione. I knew he would do it.

"I would, but I need a couple dollars to last me about a week," my mom said.

That was it. I had it with that lady. She was officially not my mom anymore. She wanted me to pay her to get me out of jail. That was the shit I was talking about.

"All right! Whatever! Just stay by the phone!" I screamed at my mom, no longer able to keep my peace.

"My mom can come. She just needs a ride. Can I call someone to pick her up?" I asked the policewoman.

"Go 'head," she said, popping her gum and flipping through a magazine.

"Thank you," I said, dialing Antione.

Pick up the phone, Ant Man, please, I thought to myself.

"It's Ant. Leave a message." *Beep.*

"Got damn it," I mumbled.

Before I could ask for one more call, the policewoman told me to go 'head.

I called my very last resort.

"Butter," I said in relief.

"Who this?" Butter asked.

"Angel. I need a huge favor."

"They locked you up?"

"Yeah. I'm down here at the police station. They goin' let me out, but I need my mom to come down here. Can you please go to her house and get her and bring her down here? I'll pay you."

There was a brief silence. Then Butter said, "Where ya mom stay at?"

"Brooklyn. Right by Louis Armstrong."

"Damn, that's a hike. You goin' definitely pay me for this. And what station they got you at?"

"In Harlem, by the river."

"Oh, yes, you owe me."

"Thank you so much, Butter. You don't know how much you are helping me right now."

I gave Butter my mom's phone number and address and then I had to return to the cell. I counted the minutes until Butter and my mom got to the station. My mom had to show her I.D., and she signed the paperwork. As soon as we stepped foot out the precinct, my mom held her hand out. I didn't have but forty dollars on me, and I wasn't about to give her my last, especially after she stole over six hundred dollars from me. She had to be crazy if she thought I would give her a dime.

"You don't gotta take me home. I got people on this side I'ma stay with tonight. Just give me that couple dollars," my mom said.

"I don't have it right now. I just got out of jail. I need time to make my money back."

My mom gave me an evil eye. "Don't play games with me, Angel! You got some money! Even if it's just a hundred dollars."

She had some nerve. *"You expect me to give you a hundred dollars after you just stole damn near ten times that from me a few days ago?"* I shouted.

"I will go in there and tell them cops to keep ya grown ass down here! I told you I needed some money . . ."

"Not no hundred dollars!"

"Well then, fifty! I don't care! I came all the way down here with no way back and . . ."

"You said you was stayin' with ya people!"

"I still need to get back tomorrow!"

Butter finally butted in, "Y'all drawin' arguin' like this in front of the police station. Angel, give ya mom some money and let's go, shit, I ain't goin' be sittin' out here all night while y'all go at each other's throats."

I took a twenty out my pocket and threw it at my mom. If it wasn't for Butter, she wouldn't have got that. But it wasn't right to have Butter standin' out there in the cold because me and my mom couldn't get it together. So I just gave her the money to shut her up. She picked the twenty up and walked off. She didn't say thank you, bye, where you goin' be stayin', or nothin'.

I followed Butter to her car up the street.

"Where am I takin' you?" Butter asked immediately after I sat in her car.

"To Antione's house in Brooklyn. Around the corner from where you picked my mom up."

"That ain't goin' work," Butter said, turning the key in the ignition.

"Why not?" I asked.

"Antione got locked up. They raided his house, too."

"What? When?"

"Do it matter? He's locked up. So where am I takin' you?"

I was dumbfounded. I didn't have an answer. I could have went back home, but it was no way in hell. I thought about Stacey and Cat. They would have probably let me stay with them for a little while, but they were still in Jamaica. And Jamal been avoiding me since that nut shit between us happened. I didn't have nowhere to go. Aunt Jackie's maybe, but I was not tryin' to go from one dope house to another.

"So?" Butter asked.

"Butter, I don't know," I whined. "I'm tryna think."

"Well, look," Butter said. "I have a extra room at my house. You can stay there if you need to, until you get on your feet."

It was goin' snow. First, Butter came through with getting my mom and bringing her to the station. Then she was offering to let me stay with her. That was surprising. I always thought she didn't like me. But I guess she was just naturally moody.

"I can?"

Butter nodded her head.

"Oh, my God. Thank you so much, Butter. That's good lookin' for real."

"Yeah. Yeah."

Butter had a brownstone in Spanish Harlem. When we pulled up, there was some guy sitting on her stoop.

"*¿Qué pasa?*" the guy said to Butter.

"What's up," Butter replied as she walked past him.

"Ju got some powder?"

"No. But I got a whole lot of pussy upstairs. What you tryna spend?"

I didn't understand what the guy wanted from Butter, but I frowned up my face at what Butter said to him. I figured she was just messing with his head, though. I walked past the guy, following Butter to her door, and he grinted on me. I rolled my eyes at his perverted-looking self.

"I got fifty bucks," he said. "for this chica right here."

"Knock on my door when you can triple that, *papí,*" Butter said, walking in her house.

Butter's house was nice and clean. It was decorated richly, with long thick curtains and tie-backs, fancy antique looking furniture, and oriental rugs. I was amazed. Butter's personality matched nothing with her home decor. It looked like the queen of England lived in that house—not a stripper named Butter.

"Butter, your house is nice," I told her.

"And it'll stay that way, too," she said.

Just then an older brown-skinned woman with big hair and too much makeup on walked down the steps. She was wearing some type of showgirl costume.

"Babe, I'm going out," the woman told Butter.

Butter told me to sit down in the living room while she walked the woman to the door.

I heard Butter ask her where she was going, and she told

Butter she wrote everything down on the board. Whatever that meant. Then I could have sworn I heard them kiss before the door opened and closed. I didn't know what to make of that. But it seemed like shit was getting stranger and stranger by the minute.

"All right. Now, this is the deal," Butter said, sitting next to me.

"I don't expect you to pay rent or buy food. But you will have to work for me if you're planning on staying here."

"Okay," I said. "What will I have to do?" Now I knew there had to be a catch somewhere. I just didn't know what. I thought maybe Butter would have wanted me to clean her house or cook her food or run her errands or something.

"I got four girls stayin' here. Most of them worked at Shake's with me when I first started there. But they got tired of workin' so damn hard for one-dollar bills. Plus a lot of them had habits and couldn't keep their rent paid, so me and Shake came up with this idea. Since he knew a lot of guys who had money and liked trickin' and I had girls at the club in line, we figured we would start a escort service."

I wanted to jump in, but I didn't. I waited for Butter to finish before I blew things out of proportion.

"Now, you'll have your own room, and like I said you won't be responsible for paying nothing. You just gotta make sure you clean up after yourself. I don't tolerate a nasty bitch. And if you got a habit, it stays in ya room. Not in my bathroom, hallway, kitchen, basement, or nowhere. It don't leave ya room or it don't come in this house, period. You'll have access to the phone, TV, and washer and dryer and pretty much make yourself at home."

All that was fine and dandy, but I was waiting to hear about the escorting part. Did she expect me to be a prostitute for her. Was she that crazy?

"As far as working for me, you'll basically make yourself available whenever I get a call for you. A guy will come pick you up and take you to the hotel around the corner. Y'all do whatever he paid for and he'll bring you back. I take my percentage off the top and you do whatever you want with yours. You don't go talkin' about what you do in the streets. You don't bring nobody here. I don't care if it's ya grand-mom. Nobody is to know where I live or what goes down in here. Last, if you get in a situation with a guy do not, under no circumstances, call 5-o. You understand?" Butter concluded.

"Butter, I don't mean to be difficult or nothing, but is there anything else I can do besides that? I mean, just until I get on my feet. I'm thinkin' I'll be stayin' here for no longer than two weeks."

"Listen. You can leave right now. I didn't tell you all that so you can debate it. That's how it is and that's how it's gonna be. I could give a fuck if you were staying for one day."

"But, Butter," I whined.

Butter cut me off, "Leave. Leave!"

"I told you in the car that I didn't have nowhere to go."

"You can go home to your mom and let her steal the draws of ya ass, or you can go sit on Antione's step until he get finish doing a dime in the feds, or you could go back down to the precinct and tell them to hold you there until your court date. You got plenty of places you can go. Now go!"

That was it. I was through with the bullshit. I felt myself giving up. I wanted a way out so bad. All I ever wanted was a way out. Why did shit have to always be so hard on me? I felt tears coming, but I fought them back. I didn't want Butter to see me cry.

"This world ain't no pretty place. You have to do what you have to do out here. And shit, it ain't no different than what you was doin' at Shake's. Pop you a E-pill if you have to. Go fuck for ten minutes, make your money, and be done with it."

A E-pill sounded good. I could use one of them. Either that or a blunt.

"You got one?" I asked Butter.

"E?"

"Yeah."

"Not on me, but I can get you some."

"What about some weed?" I asked, desperately wanting to numb the pain I was feeling.

"Oh, I got some weed. That's probably what you need, too," Butter said, getting up from the couch. "Come on."

I walked up the flight of stairs behind Butter. She led me into a back room. It was small but very neat. It had a twin bed in it that was made with fresh-looking sheets. It had a TV in it, too. It was perfect for me. I knew I could get comfortable there. As far as escorting, or whatever, fuck it. I chose not to think about it at that time. I really just wanted to clear my head and get some rest.

Butter handed me a bag of weed and a blunt.

"Calm ya nerves," she said as she left the room and closed the door behind her.

And that was all she wrote.

Long Ways from Home

Yo! Angel! Yo! Get up!" I heard Butter call out.

I pulled the blanket from over my eyes. The sun shone bright through the small window in the room. I had to squint to see Butter.

"Huh?" I asked.

"You pregnant?" Butter asked abruptly.

"Huh?" All I could think was what is she trippin' about today.

Every day it was something different with Butter. If I ain't know better I would have thought she was bipolar. You never knew what to expect from her. But I learned that no matter how green the grass grew it was always horseshit that grew it.

"Are . . . you . . . pregnant?" Butter said slowly, as if she was spelling something out for me.

"No! Why?"

" 'Cause for the past three days all you've done was eat and sleep."

Butter was right. I had only been eating and sleeping. But for some reason my body felt very exhausted. I guessed it was from stress.

"Butter, I just been tired, that's all. I been through a lot. I guess my body needed a rest," I told her.

"Well, I let you rest long enough. Tonight I'm takin' you out."

"You heard from Shake?" I asked her, avoiding her comment.

"Yeah. But Shake isn't your concern. Angel is."

"Did he hear from Antione?"

Butter rolled her eyes. "Neither Shake nor Antione can get you out of working tonight. Both of them is locked up, and both of them lookin' at some time. It's no secret that they deal, and the feds been watchin' them for a while. They knew it. I knew it. We all knew it. Now, I know Ant is like a brother to you, but he ain't here to save you. Now, I ran down the rules the night you stepped foot through my door, and just because I ain't enforced 'em since you got here, don't mean that they changed. I called myself being nice. And you can try to take my kindness for weakness if you want to."

"Butter, I asked about Antione 'cause I just wanted to know. I'm not tryna to argue with you."

"Good," Butter said. "Get up. I wanna introduce you to the other girls. They can show you the ropes."

Butter walked out the room, practically slamming the door.

Drama mama, I thought. Got damn, she was a hell-raiser. I forced myself out the bed. I felt so sluggish. I wondered even, was it more to my sleepiness than stress. I've been stressed out before and never felt like that. I slipped on the only pair of jeans I had with me and walked out into the hall. Butter was standing at the doorway of the room next to mine. She used her finger to tell me to come to her.

"Angel, this is Mary. Mary, this is Angel."

Mary was a skinny white woman, and if she wasn't in her late forties something had definitely taken its toll on her. I wouldn't have been surprised if it was Butter.

"Hey," she said softly with a half smile.

"Hi," I spoke back shyly. I felt so uncomfortable. It seemed like I was surrounded by a bunch of psychos. The woman, who I assumed was Butter's girlfriend, with the showgirl getup, Mary, and especially Butter—they all seemed so sneaky and shady. I felt like I had to watch my back and not in a minor way either, but in a way like I didn't want to eat anything they cooked and I definitely wasn't about to smoke nothing Butter gave me ever again. And when I thought about it, that was probably why I was feeling so lazy. Butter probably fucked around and gave me some laced weed.

I wasn't the least bit interested in meeting Mary, or any of the other girls for that matter. I didn't know them. And I didn't have any intentions on getting to know them. The way I was feeling there at Butter's house I'd rather stayed back with my mom. At least then, I would be with Naja and Kindle. They needed me, and I had been feeling guilty since I left them. Butter didn't know it, but my mind was made up. I was leaving her house and going back to Brooklyn.

Butter had went out to make a run. I was in the house with Mary and one other girl named Karryn, who hardly spoke English. I figured that was the perfect time to leave. I mean, it wasn't like I couldn't have left while Butter was there, but to avoid any confrontation, the best time was then. I washed up, got dressed, and rolled out.

I hadn't been outside in a few days, and the fresh air on my face felt good. It wasn't really cold outside so I walked to the subway instead of taking a cab. I caught the D train to Dekalb and got on the 52 bus going toward my way. As I got closer to my mom's house I started thinking that I should have called first. I wasn't in the mood for any surprises. I got off the bus at the corner. C&S's was closed. *Now, see, Cat would have never had that store closed on a Monday afternoon,* I thought. *They better bring their behinds back here to the States if they wanna stay in business.*

I walked down my block and it looked different, like it had been years instead of days since I been there. From the top of the block it looked like one of the houses had caught on fire. The top windows were burned out. I felt a panic come over me as I got closer. It looked like Jamal's house. I started to walk fast to see if it was or not and hoped it wasn't.

Oh, my God. It was my house. I ran up on the porch. The

door was padlocked. The front window was boarded up and there were some burned pieces of furniture on the curb that the trash men needed to collect. *Oh, my God,* I thought. *How did this happen?* I stood there in front of my house with my hands over my mouth. I almost cried, going over all the what-ifs in my head. I knocked on Jamal's door. I didn't care that he was mad at me. I needed some information. Nobody answered. *Aunt Jackie,* I thought.

✽

I practically ran to Aunt Jackie's house. "Aunt Jackie, it's me, Angel!" I yelled through the door, out of breath.

Aunt Jackie opened the door, sipping a beer. "My, my, my, look what the wind blew in."

I went in Aunt Jackie's house and sat down on her sofa.

"Aunt Jackie, where my mom and them at? I went around the house and it's burned up," I asked, fearing the worst.

"Oh, child, you ain't heard? Your mom's house caught on fire."

"I know that. But what happened? Where's Naja and Kenny?"

Aunt Jackie sipped the beer and explained, "That damn Marvin fell asleep with a cigarette lit. He got up and flames and smoke was everywhere. He made it out just in time. It was a good thing the kids weren't there."

I sighed in relief. "Aunt Jackie, where are they stayin'?" I asked for the hundredth time.

"Oh, they at some shelter. I got the address written down

somewhere around here," she said as she walked over and opened the china closet in the dining room.

She sipped her beer again then set it on the dining room table. Then she started going through papers and mail. "I know I wrote it down somewhere," she mumbled.

"When was the fire? I just seen my mom the other night."

"Oh, yeah, that night she went and got you out of jail?"

"She told you that?"

"Yeah. You know your mom can't keep nothin' to herself. Yeah, that was the night it happened," Aunt Jackie said.

"Matter fact, it was a good thing you got locked up 'cause had your mom not had to go get you she wouldn't have brought those kids over here and they would have all been in that house when it caught fire. Humph. Ain't that nothin'. Oh, here it is," Aunt Jackie muffled, holding an envelope in her hand.

I stood up and took the envelope. "Thank you, Aunt Jackie."

"No, no, no," Aunt Jackie said. "You better copy it down somewhere. I need that."

"Oh," I said, digging in my pocket for a pen.

I wrote down the information and left. It said that they were in a battered women's shelter. I wanted to see them so bad. I was mad at myself that Naja and Kindle had to go through that without me. I was thankful, though, that they weren't in the house. I did a lot of thinking on the bus ride to the shelter. I definitely wasn't going back to Butter's. I needed to get myself together and be with my sister and brother. For a minute I was giving up on them, smoking to get my mind off them, but I had to stop all that. I told myself that from that day forth I would stick it out with them. I didn't want to keep runnin'. And it seemed like I was only runnin' backward anyway.

When I got to the shelter it was actually a church. I went inside and there was an elderly woman at the front desk.

"Hi, can I help you with something?" she asked me, looking at me over the top of her glasses instead of through her glasses.

"Yes," I said as I walked over to her. "My house had caught on fire and my aunt had told me that my mom and my sister and brother were staying here."

"What's your mom's name, hon?" she asked, looking through a notebook.

"Carmina Washington."

"Washington," she mumbled, dragging her finger slowly down the page.

"And what's your name?"

"Angel. Angel Washington."

"Well, it says here that Carmina Washington has two kids. Naja Washington and Kindle, or Kindle Washington. It don't say nothing about a Angel. Are you her blood relative?"

"Yes. I'm her oldest daughter. It's just that I wasn't home at the time," I explained, wishing she would just get her old ass up and call my mom to the front or something.

"Well, let me call my supervisor and see what she says, okay?"

"Okay." *Thank you,* I thought. *That's what you should have done from jump.*

The lady picked up the phone receiver and dialed some numbers.

"Kathy, It's me, Eleanor. There's a young lady here looking for one of the residents. She says she's her daughter, but she's not listed as a resident."

Duh, I wasn't here when they got here, I thought as I rolled my eyes.

"Yes. Carmina Washington. It says here that she has two children—Naja and Kindle. No, her name is Angel. Okay. Okay," the lady said. Then she looked up at me over the top of her glasses again. "She put me on hold. She's going to go get Carmina."

I nodded my head, relieved that somebody had some sense.

After a short while, the lady started talking back on the phone, but mostly just answering yes and no. She hung up and said to me, "My supervisor spoke with the resident, and she said she only has the two kids that are here on the list. Are you sure you're her blood relative?" the lady asked me, as if I wouldn't know that.

I backed away from the desk and left the church without saying a word. I didn't want that lady to see me cry, and I knew that tears were coming. Outside on the church steps, I couldn't hold back. I sat down and put my face in my lap. I cried like a baby. It was getting colder as night was setting in. I was trying to figure out where I would stay. I wished Stacey and Cat were back. I wished Antione didn't get locked up. I wished I never messed things up with Jamal. My last resort was Aunt Jackie's house. I got up off the steps and walked to the bus. I used my last couple dollars for the fare and went back around my way.

I got to Aunt Jackie's door and her oldest son Hasaan was going in.

"What's up, Angel? Where you been at, ma?" Hasaan asked me.

"Around," I said with a smile on my face. I didn't want him to know that I was upset. The minute I showed weakness to him or any man, as far as I was concerned, I was bound to be taken advantage of.

"You comin' here?" he asked as he held the screen door open for me.

"Yeah."

I walked in Aunt Jackie's house. The lights were dim in the living room, but you could see that it was filthy. A pile of dirty clothes were on one sofa and blankets and a pillow on the other, and beer cans decorated the table and entertainment center.

"Mom!" Hasaan called upstairs. "Angel down here!" Then he turned to me and said, "She up there. You can go up there if you want. I'm about to go down in the basement. You can turn on the TV. The remote over there."

"Angel!" Aunt Jackie's loud drunken voice bounced off the walls.

Aunt Jackie walked down the steps in a dingy tan robe. She

had a scarf on her head and some flip-flops on her ashy feet. She was scratching like she had fleas. She looked so funky. I held my breath when she hugged me.

"What you doin' back here?" she asked, smiling with those saggy lips that people get when they drink too much.

"I couldn't find the shelter," I lied.

"Oh, child, you been living in Brooklyn ya whole life and don't know ya way around the block! Ain't that nothin'," Aunt Jackie rambled. "So what, you wanna stay here?"

I nodded my head—although it wasn't that I wanted to stay there, it was just that I had no choice if I didn't want to go back to Butter's house.

Aunt Jackie started picking up the dirty clothes off the sofa. "Well, that's fine. I don't know why you actin' all shy like you ain't family. Let me get these clothes up. Kareem put his dirty shit on my couch. I keep tellin' him this ain't no hamper."

I watched Aunt Jackie clean off what I figured would be my bed. Tears formed in my eyes as I envisioned my mom telling some lady that she only had two kids. I tried to block it out my mind by telling myself I didn't care, but that didn't work. Instead it made me feel worse. I felt unwanted. It seemed the more I tried to convince myself that what my mom did didn't matter to me, the more hurt I felt.

"I'll bring down some sheets and a cover for you. I don't believe you couldn't find that shelter. It's right up there on what's-a-name," Aunt Jackie said as she walked up the steps carrying the load of clothes.

With the clothes gone, I could see what looked like piss stains on the sofa cushions. I was not about to sleep on that. Butter may have been shady, but at least her house was clean. And anyway, I needed to make some money—and if Butter's house was my only means to do that then I had to go back. I had rather deal with Butter's mood swings than sleep on a pissy couch.

"Aunt Jackie!" I yelled up the steps.

"I'm comin', Angel! Got damn! I'm getting you some blankets!" she yelled back.

"No. That's all right! I'm going over my friend house!" I told her, and I left.

It was dark by then. I didn't have any money so I had no choice but to call Butter. I was not about to walk to Harlem, and hitchhiking was out of the question. I went to the pay phone and called Butter collect.

"Butter," I said in a hurry.

"You better be in jail calling my house collect!" Butter snapped.

"Butter, I went to get some clothes from my mom's house and it had caught on fire the other day so I was at every shelter looking for my mom and them all day. I used all my money on bus fare. I need a ride back to your house," I explained as fast and simple as I could.

"Oh, really? Okay. Where you at?"

"My mom block."

"All right. Stay right there," Butter said. Then right before she hung up, I heard her say, "I got something for her ass."

I put the phone back on the receiver and went inside the Chinese store at the end of my mom's block.

"Can I help you?" the short Asian woman asked a lady who was already in the store.

"Yeah. Give me three wings with salt, pepper, and hot sauce, and a loosie," the lady said.

I sat down on the window seat and watched every passing car, anticipating my ride.

"You Carmina daughter, ain't you?" the lady asked me.

I turned to look at her. She was kind of heavy, light brown skin with a lot of bumps on her face. She had on a baseball cap and a leather jacket.

"Yeah," I answered her, trying to figure out if I knew her and where from.

"You look just like ya motha," she went on. "I'm Nina. I used to baby-sit you and ya brotha when y'all was real little. You probably don't remember me, though, 'cause you was a baby. How ya mom doin'?"

"She all right," I said, unwilling to tell her my business.

"I ain't seen Carmina in years. The last time I seen her, you was like one and ya brotha Curtis was like eight or nine. How he doin'? I bet you he a grown ass momma's boy ain't he?"

"He got killed," I burst her bubble.

"Oh, no, get out of here. When?" she asked, dragging her words.

"Two years ago," I told her.

"Oh, my God. Damn, see I been down South for ten years, and I was locked up for a while before that so I'm like out of the loop, you know. But damn, I am sorry."

"It's all right," I said.

"Damn, that's fucked up. Curt. Damn, wait 'til I tell my motha. My motha loved her some Curt. I had y'all all the time. Y'all was like my kids, especially Curtis. He used to play with my nephew," she reflected.

"Three wings," the Asian woman spoke through the thick glass, interrupting Nina.

"Well, it was good seeing you. Angel, right?"

"Yeah."

"I'm sorry about ya brotha, too. But listen, take down my numba," she said. "Can I see that pen?" she asked the Asian woman.

She scribbled her phone number on a piece of the brown bag her food was in and gave it to me. Then she stuck the loose cigarette she bought behind her ear.

"Tell ya mom to call me. I'm back up here for a while. And take care of yaself, all right?"

"Yeah," I said, watching the lady leave.

She had to bring up my brother, didn't she. I was not in the mood for memories. That made me want to cry all over again. Just as I looked back out the window, I saw a car driving slowly down the block. It didn't look like Butter's car, though. But I went outside to check. She could have sent one of the girls to get me, and I was not tryin' to miss my ride.

Beep! Beep! The car horn sounded. I walked slowly toward the car, and the window rolled down. A guy was driving.

"You Angel?"

I nodded my head.

"Butter sent me to pick you up," he said.

I hesitated.

"I'm supposed to be taking you to her house," he elaborated.

I didn't know who he was, but Butter sent him, so I got in his car.

"I'm Bruce," he introduced himself. "What you doin' walkin' the streets in this cold weather?"

I ignored him. I wasn't interested in having a conversation with him. I just wanted to get to Butter's.

"You not talkin' to me?" he asked.

"I'm just tired," I responded, trying to give him a hint.

"Is that right?" he asked, pulling the car into a parking space a couple blocks from where he picked me up. "Well, we can make this quick, then."

I looked at him, confused. "What are you talkin' about?"

He started unbuckling his belt.

"Hold on. What are you doin'?"

He returned a confused expression to me and said, "You do work for Butter, don't you?"

I didn't answer that question.

He proceeded, "She told me I was picking up a date. I didn't come all the way on this end for nothin'."

"I thought you was coming to take me to her house," I told him.

"Yeah, after you, you know," he said vaguely.

I frowned my face up. "Are you serious?"

"Look, Butter and me been knowing each other for a long time. I send her plenty business. And she look out for me in return. Now, ya ride home is all I have to pay for a nice time. So, what's it goin' be? You wanna ride or not?"

I let what he said sink in, and in the process I remembered hearing Butter say she had something for my ass when we hung up the phone. I put two and two together and that was what she was talking about. She had some shit with her, I thought. But it was what it was. I sucked up what was left of my pride and dignity and gave the man what he was looking for.

Back at Butter's house, Mary was cooking something that smelled good. I didn't know that a skinny woman like her knew what cooking was. I sat down in the kitchen and laid my head down on the table. Mary carried on as if I never walked in.

In no time Butter appeared at the doorway. "So, you wandered off and realized you ain't have nowhere to go? Well, I hope you learned a lesson. You could have made a hundred dollars off that blow job, but what you get? A ride. All you gotta do is stay in your place and play your position. Grow up, little girl! And grow up fast!"

I sat at the kitchen table and thought to myself, *One of these days Butter is goin' to make me hurt her.* The only reason why I hadn't checked Butter up to that point was because I knew I needed her. But as soon as I found my way out of that position, she had better believe we was goin' brawl.

"Mary, what you smoke?" I asked, trying to take my mind off the bullshit I had went through that day.

Mary didn't answer my question. She just looked at me with that same warning expression on her face. But who was she to judge? It was clear she was no saint. I knew she smoked something, so I didn't know why she gave me that look like I asked her something foreign.

"What, you deaf?" I asked her with an attitude. I was mad and she was the only person I could get away with taking my anger out on. "I asked you what you smoke?"

She rolled her eyes at me.

"Bitch! I ain't goin' ask you again!" I said, standing up. I wanted to walk over to that stove and dump Mary's pale bony face in the pot of boiling water.

Mary rolled her eyes at me again and still did not answer me. That was it. Somebody was going to get their ass kicked, and Mary was in the wrong place at the wrong time so it was bound to be her. I walked over to Mary and stood right in her face. She was a few inches taller than me, so it was like I was talking to her neck.

"Did you hear what the fuck I said? What the fuck do you smoke?!" I didn't even wait for an answer that time. I was so frustrated I grabbed Mary's long neck with both of my hands and squeezed as hard as I could. She grabbed my arms and tried to take them off her. I didn't budge. I just squeezed tighter. Her white face turned red and veins popped out of her head. Still I squeezed. Her grip on my arms loosened and her eyes were opening and closing.

"ANGEL!" Butter's voice rang out.

I suddenly released my hold on Mary and she dropped to the kitchen floor. I turned to look at Butter, and she was fuming. She ran up on me and gripped me by my hair. She threw me up against the wall and started choking me.

"NOW, HOW DO YOU LIKE IT?!" she shouted.

If I would have been able to talk I would have told her not to stop. I was losing my breath, but I didn't care. I wanted Butter to choke me to death. That would have made my day.

"If I ever catch you doin' some shit like that in my house again I'm goin' beat ya ass and then let every bitch in here beat ya ass. You hear me?" she shouted as she took her hands from around my neck.

I used the wall to hold myself up as I gasped for air. I wanted to punch Butter in the face, but I maintained my self-control. And I didn't think it was because I needed Butter either, because after she choked me I could have cared less about that. I was scared of Butter. Since the day I met her I was intimidated by her. But that night in her kitchen, it was no longer intimidation but fear. The look in her eyes when she had her hands around my neck was enough to make me pass out, let alone my loss of oxygen.

"Go upstairs and wash ya face and ya pussy. You wanna act a fool in my house, it's time you pay some bills around this mothafucka!" Butter said to me with a disgusted look on her face.

It was a little after eleven when Butter drove me to a dark block under a bridge in uptown Manhattan. There were all these girls out there, at least a dozen, half naked, hoppin' in and out of cars. My nerves were shot and I was sure Butter could tell, because she turned to me and gave me some E-pills.

"Here, take these."

I was so happy to see them little blue pills. I popped them in my mouth like they were candy.

"I'm goin' let you out here. Stand on that corner or that corner," she instructed, pointing to the two corners she restricted me to. "When a car roll up, you go up to the passenger window and ask the driver how can you help him. Just like you work at McDonald's or some shit. Just say How can I help you? But say it in a sexy way. Make it sound sweet. If he ask about prices tell 'im they the best he goin' get and ask 'im if he ever dealt with Butter. If he say yeah, he'll already know the cost and tell you to get in. If he say no, tell 'im he don't know what he missin' and walk away from his car. Don't get in a car if the trick say he don't know Butter. Not on ya first night, anyway. I'm goin' be parked right here the whole time. If you need me, don't call me or yell. Just walk ya ass over here or flag me down," Butter ran things down to me.

I listened, but I didn't really hear her. I was purposely ignoring her. I was starting to feel the effects of the Ecstasy for one, and for two, I hated Butter's guts at that point. I wasn't tryin' to hear shit she had to say. She leaned over me and opened my door. I got out and walked about a half block down the street to one of the corners Butter told me to stand on. My knees were shaking so bad I barely made it down there. I noticed all eyes were on me and that made me even more nervous. No sooner than I got on the corner did a chick approach me.

"You got a light?" the short, thick, light-skinned woman asked me, sounding like Rosie Perez.

Before I could say no she looked me in my eyes and said,

"You high as giraffe pussy, baby girl. You shouldn't be out here like that. A trick'll take more than you tryna give if he see you on like that," she explained.

I looked at her and smiled.

"And you a baby, too?" she went on. "Dat ain't right. Butter don't got no shame, do she? Got little kids out here. This ain't no place for no kids and she know that shit, too."

"You know Butter?" I asked her, still smiling.

She shook her head and glanced up the street at Butter's car. "Yeah, and just so you know, she don't play by the rules. You better watch ya back," the woman said before she walked over to another girl and got a light from her.

Cars continued to ride by. Some stopped and picked up a girl and others just drove on by. The corners were getting emptier as time went on. Girls were jumpin' in those cars. I knew Butter was watching me, and it was probably only a matter of time before she was going to drive down the street and tell me I better be just like them bitches and jump my ass in one of those cars. I could see her saying it just like that, too. I smiled at the thought of Butter's spiteful ass. Then a car pulled up right on me.

"You smilin' at me, sexy?" the old man asked.

He looked like he was somebody's great-grandfather. He was toothless and all.

"What it take to get you home with me?" he asked.

I glanced up the street at Butter's car and could imagine her telling me, Get ya ass in that car.

"It take a whole lot of Butter," I said, trying to remember the script Butter told me.

"Oh, is that right? You one of Butter's girls? Well, I got what you need. Get in."

I opened the passenger door and sat on the torn leather seats. The inside of the car smelled like cigars. There was some slow music playing that I didn't recognize. The old man was humming to the beat in between talking to me.

"You a fresh face. I love me a fresh face," he said. "You look kind of young. You suck dick?"

I looked at the man and wanted to throw up. He looked old enough to be my mom's dad and was asking me if I sucked dick.

"You don't talk much, huh? Well, that's fine with me. Save ya mouth for what I'm payin' you for. I been waitin' all week for this. And I done hit the jackpot and got me a baby. I think the youngest I had was like twenty-two. What, you like eighteen?"

I was high, but I wasn't crazy and it was no way I was sucking that old man's dick. I figured if I told him how old I was he would be like *Oh no, you too young,* and drop me off.

"Fifteen," I responded.

His eyes lit up. A smile appeared on his face.

"Fifteen? Oh, I really hit the jackpot! A old man like me havin' a little pretty thing like you suckin' my dick. I'm about to pull over right now. Forget goin' to the motel," he said.

That wasn't the response I was looking for, but I shouldn't have been surprised. Old nasty-ass men like him liked young girls. He reminded me of an older version of Marvin, and I couldn't take it no more. As soon as he pulled over to the curb, I opened the door and got out.

"Yo! What you doin'?" he yelled out the car window.

I ignored him and walked up the three to four blocks back to the corner he picked me up from. I knew Butter was going to have something to say, but I didn't care. I wasn't sucking that man's dick.

Just as I predicted, Butter's car came driving down to the corner. She barely put it in park before she jumped out. She held her hand out as if she wanted me to put something in it. "Where my money?"

"I didn't do anything with him," I told her nonchalantly. I was trying to keep from making a scene.

"Why not?" Butter asked, agitated.

I wanted to tell Butter to pipe down before she had a heart attack, but that would have added fuel to her fire. "He was givin' me the runaround, so I told him to let me out," I lied.

Pop! Butter smacked the shit out of me. Between the cold air and the stinging sensation from the smack, it felt like my face was broken. I couldn't even cry, she hit me so hard. I was stunned.

"Listen, to me! You are pushin' so many limits! If you weren't Antione's peoples I would've fed you to the wolves. But keep playin' games wit me, and Antione or no Antione I'ma show you a side of me you goin' wish you never had to see. Now, the next car that come through here you better hop ya ass in and do whatever he tell you to do. I wouldn't care if he asked to ass fuck you in the middle of Times Square. You got that? Now, play with me if you want!" Butter told me. She got in her car and drove around the block.

In the meantime, the couple other girls out there were

staring at me whispering among themselves. I was standing frozen on the corner, scared to death. A car rode up, and I don't know how, but I managed to walk over to the passenger side.

"Can I help you?" I asked, sticking to Butter's script.

The well-groomed man looked at me with sorrow and told me to get in.

"What you want? A blow job? You wanna fuck me?" I asked, wanting to get the whole thing done and over with. My heart was racing and my head was spinning. I wished I had blacked out or at least had some weed. I was so paranoid I forgot to ask him if he knew Butter.

"I wanna talk," the guy said as he pulled off from the corner.

"We can do whatever you want. Long as you pay me. Long as I put some money in that bitch hand," I poured.

I couldn't help myself any longer. My leg started to shake. I was hurt. My spirits were broken. I was losing myself.

"Listen, I'm an outreach counselor," the guy began. "I help girls like yourself get off the streets."

I cut him off, "All that's fine. But to be honest, I don't have time to talk right now unless you're going to pay me."

"I'm not here for sex, though."

"Okay! Well, let me out! I am wastin' my time with you, and if I go back there with no money she goin' kick my ass!"

"I want to help you," the guy said. "Take my card. Give me a call. You don't have to do this."

Tears poured down my face. The man didn't have a clue

what was going to happen if I walked back to that corner with no money in my hand.

"You wanna help me? Then give me some money. Anything! Just so I can pay her. Please. I will do whatever you want me to."

The guy pulled into a parking space and took a business card from his glove compartment. He handed it to me, and I put it in my back pocket.

"I can't give you any money. That's against policy. But, I can help you. Call me . . ."

I got out of his car and slammed his door. *"Jackass!"* I screamed at him. I couldn't believe my luck. The time I was going to do something, the nigga wasn't a trick. Butter was going to whip my ass. I knew she wouldn't be tryna to hear that he was some fuckin' outreach counselor. She was goin' be like *Bullshit, you just didn't want to do shit with him,* or she was goin' ask me did he say he knew her. Either way she was goin' to be pissed off 'cause I fucked up.

I walked up the street. But that time I didn't reach the corner. Butter sped up on me about a block before. Her brakes screeched, drawing attention to her. I saw a few people looking in our direction, including the Rosie Perez–sounding woman.

Butter jumped out the car and grabbed me by my shirt. "Why do you want me to hurt you?" she asked.

"Butter, I swear to God on my brother that the guy wasn't a trick. I told him I would do whatever . . ."

Butter cut me off, "He wasn't a trick? I been workin' these

corners for three years and every mothafucka that come through here and pick a bitch up is a trick! Now, you goin' bullshit me? The first time it's shame on you. But the second time it's shame on me. And I ain't about to let no ho shame me!" Butter hauled off and smacked me again. That time my nose bled. I was scared for my life. From the corner of my eye I could see people approaching us.

One was the man who got me in trouble in the first place.

"Yo! Yo! Yo!" he shouted out to Butter. "Leave her alone! I'm calling the cops," he said, jogging toward us with his cell phone in his hand.

Butter let me go and started to walk back to her car.

"You lucky this clown is callin' the law! But you gotta come home! And if you do, you better not be empty-handed. I'll cut ya fuckin' throat!"

Butter got in her car and sped off. I stood there shaking frantically. I didn't even know how I was still standing because I couldn't feel my legs.

"You want me to take you to the police station," the guy asked, dialing numbers in his phone.

I shook my head no. They would have locked me up or put me in some group home somewhere.

"What about the hospital?"

"No! Got damn it!" I snapped. "I told you how you could've helped me and you didn't so get the fuck out of my face!"

"I got her," Rosie Perez sound-alike said.

The woman wrapped her arm around my shivering body.

Her touch made me jump. I had never been so scared in my life. I was shaking and crying uncontrollably. The few people that were out were gathered around looking at me like I was a nut case. The woman started walking me back up to the corner.

"You sure? I can give y'all a ride somewhere," the man insisted.

"No, that's okay," the woman said.

"Well, can I call somebody for you?" He wouldn't give up.

"*Noooo!*" I finally yelled. Then my body went into convulsions. I started screaming, "I CAN'T TAKE THIS SHIT NO MORE!"

I had a nervous breakdown. It was on the ho strip under the bridge in uptown Manhattan. Long ways from home.

Love the One You're With

he smell of bacon and eggs woke me from a deep sleep. When I opened my eyes I didn't know where the hell I was. I crawled from under the Dora the Explorer sheets and comforter and sat up in the twin-size bed. I scanned the room to gain familiarity, and the pink and purple walls and Dora everything did not ring any bells. I almost had a heart attack when I looked over at the doorway and saw three small children smiling at me.

"Oh, my God. Y'all scared me," I said holding my chest. "I didn't know y'all were there."

I was talking to these kids like I knew who they were.

"Mommy, she's woke!" the biggest one yelled. She couldn't be no older than six or seven. Her two front teeth were missing, but she was adorable. She was light-skinned, almost yellow, with green eyes and dark blond hair that was platted down her back. Her fat cheeks made me want to pinch them so bad.

The other two kids were little boys. One looked like he was four or five and the other about three, Kindle's age. They were chubby, too, with the same complexion, eye color, and hair color as the girl.

As I was getting out of the bed, another unfamiliar face appeared.

"Do you want some breakfast?" the short, stocky woman asked.

I knew that voice from somewhere, I thought. I smiled and said, "No, thank you," even though I was starved and wanted to run down the steps and stuff my face with every bit of whatever she had cooked. The thing was I wasn't sure who she was and where I knew her from. But I knew that Rosie Perez voice.

"You don't remember me, do you?" she asked, assuming correctly.

"Not really," I said, smiling, hoping not to offend her.

"I met you last night. You were having some problems with the girl, Butter," she refreshed my memory.

"Ohhhh," I said. Her asking me for a light popped in my head. "I remember."

"Come on downstairs and get you something to eat. You need to put something in your stomach. You had a rough night."

"Okay," I said as I started to make up the bed I had slept in.

"Leave those covers the way they are, and come eat this food before it gets cold," the woman instructed.

"You sure?" I asked, minding my manners.

"Yeah. Come on and eat."

"Okay, I'll be right down," I said. "I gotta use the bathroom."

"It's right there to your right," she told me and headed back down the steps.

I went into the small bathroom, and if I wasn't wide awake by then the bright yellow color scheme would have surely done the job. Everything from the shower curtain, bath towels, and window shades to the rugs, trash can, and soap dish was sunshine yellow.

After I went to the bathroom I flushed the toilet and washed my hands. I looked in the mirror and my lip was swollen. *"How the hell did that happen,"* I thought aloud. I touched my lip gently and tried to remember how it got like that. I figured it had to have something to do with Butter, because I didn't wake up at her house and plus the lady told me I was having problems with her.

I went downstairs, and it was clearer to me that the lady loved bright colors. I had to walk through a bright orange living and dining room to make it to the bright green kitchen.

"Good morning," I said, as I sat down at the kitchen table.

"Good afternoon," the lady replied, as she put scoops of food onto a plate and placed it in the microwave.

"What time is it?" I was curious.

"Twelve thirty. You slept pretty late," she said, turning to face me.

I wanted to ask her some questions, but I didn't know her name. I had been in that lady's house, slept in her child's bed, and was about to eat her food, and didn't know what to call her. I felt bad. "I'm sorry," I said. "What's your name again? I can't remember last night too good."

"That's okay. I didn't even tell you my name last night. But anyway, I'm Elaine. And these are my children, Brianna, Bryan, and Brandon."

"Oh, I'm Angel," I said.

"Say hi to Ms. Angel," Elaine told her kids as she took the plate of food out of the microwave and placed it on the table in front of me.

"Hi, Ms. Angel." Brianna did what she was told. Bryan and Brandon mumbled hi under their breath.

I smiled at them and spoke back. Then I thanked Elaine for the eggs, bacon, and home fries and dug in.

I was so hungry I ate like a pig. I didn't even care that Brianna was staring at me, smiling as if I was a life-size toy she was dying to play with.

After I filled my stomach up some and got a little comfortable, I decided I would grill Elaine.

"What happened last night?" I asked.

Elaine made Brianna move out of the chair across from me. "Go in the living room with your brothers or something," she told her daughter.

"Baby girl, you were out of it. I thought you were going to

faint. I just put you in a taxi and brought you here. I didn't wanna leave you out there 'cause Butter was talkin' about cuttin' ya throat and that guy you had went with was threatenin' to call the cops. I felt sorry for you 'cause I knew you were in over ya head. You ain't but what, sixteen?"

"I'll be sixteen next year."

"So you're only fifteen? Girl, when I was fifteen I was in school thinking about what I was going to wear to the dance. What are you doin' out there on the strip?" Elaine seemed concerned.

I shrugged my shoulders.

"What do you mean you don't know? You don't have no business out there like that. You know how dangerous it is out there. And then you dealing with Butter? She is throwed off, you know that, right? Everybody know it. She belong in a mental hospital. She be snappin' on girls left and right, gettin' them hooked on drugs and shit so she can have more control over them. She put one of her girls in the hospital before. The girl was fucked up. She ain't good people at all, mommy. You don't need to be nowhere near her. How did you get down with her in the first place?"

I shook my head and said, "It's a long story. I met her at a club."

"Shake's?" Elaine was on point.

"Yeah."

Elaine shook her head. "Um, um, um," she said. "Shake and Butter still takin' advantage of girls. See, I got out there around the same time as Butter. Shake was her pimp back then, and he pretty much schooled her on how to control and make money off of young naive girls like you," Elaine explained. "She was trying to get me on her team at one point. But, I was like no. 'Cause first of all, I was older and I didn't plan on being out there long. I planned to get in and get out. 'Cause see, I wasn't never like a stripper or a drug addict or nothing like that, like most of the girls on the strip. My situation was different. My husband was the breadwinner. He was a Wall Street broker and he took good care of us. But he had got murdered. They had robbed him at gunpoint and murdered him," Elaine recollected.

"I'm so sorry to hear that," I told her.

"Oh, it's okay. It's been like four years now. I done dealt with it, you know. But, at the time, it was crazy because I was pregnant with my youngest, Brandon. And I didn't have no job or no skills and all I had was a diploma—and with the high bills we had, I needed more than minimum wage. So a friend of mine who I used to hang out with before I got married had told me about how I could make fast, easy money. At first I was like hell no, you know. But then when those bills started piling up and I was looking at my babies like I can't have my kids in no shelter, I was like hell, I gotta do it. But like I said, I was planning on getting in and out. I thought I could do it just to make enough money to carry me until I could get some college credits and get a good job. But that plan went south. School was hard. Especially with three kids."

I listened to Elaine tell me her story and I felt for her. She seemed like a nice, well-to-do lady and I could imagine how it was to have a good life with her husband and kids and then have it all taken away in a tragedy like that. That was just how it happened with me in terms of my brother. Before he was killed we had a good life. My mom wasn't strung out and we were straight. So, I knew where Elaine was coming from.

"So, what's your story?" Elaine asked. "Where's your mother? And what you running the streets for?"

"Blaaah. Blaaah."

"Oh, my goodness, Angel, are you okay?" Elaine jumped up and got paper towels from the roll.

"I am so sorry," I managed to say, wiping my mouth. I had spit up all on Elaine's kitchen floor. I didn't know why. I didn't even feel it coming. It just crept up on me.

"It's okay. It's just food," Elaine said, as she laid paper towels over my vomit.

I stood up to get more, and I felt so dizzy I had to sit back down. I rested my head in my hands.

Elaine stopped what she was doing and looked at me. "Angel, are you all right?"

"I feel nauseous," I told her.

"What were you high off last night?"

I didn't want to admit to Elaine that I had been high off anything, but the way I was feeling, I thought it was best to tell the truth, just in case I needed to go to the hospital or something.

"Ecstasy."

"Was that your first time taking it?"

"No."

"Well, have you ever felt like this before afterward?"

"No."

"Hmm," Elaine pondered. "Are you pregnant?"

"No."

"You a virgin?"

"No."

"Well, how do you know you're not pregnant? When was your last period?"

I thought back to my last period and calculated the days in my head. *It went off around the end of October. So it had to come on like a week before that.*

"Around October twenty-something."

"So, you should have gotten it again around November twenty-something. Did you?"

I shook my head.

"Well, you need to get a pregnancy test. That's the only thing I can think of."

I felt so bad I wasn't really listening to what Elaine was saying. I heard her, but I wasn't listening to her. She walked over and got a bottle of Pine-Sol from the cabinet under the sink. Then she picked up a small mop bucket and placed it in the sink. She opened the Pine-Sol and poured it in the bucket while she ran water in with it. The smell quickly filled the air. I got up from the chair and tried to make it over to the trash can in time, but I was too late. I spit up again.

"Oh, yeah, you're pregnant," Elaine said confidently.

✴

I was asleep in bed when Elaine got back from the store with a pregnancy test. She woke me up and explained to me what I had to do. I went in the bathroom and followed the instructions. I prayed that no line would appear. While I waited the couple minutes, I thought about the last time Jamal and me did it. I was trying to remember if we used a condom. I wasn't sure. We used them sometimes. But other times we just did it and he pulled out. I couldn't remember if the last time was one of those pull-out times or not. I prayed it was a condom time, though.

Knock, knock. "You all right in there?"

I cracked open the bathroom door, and Elaine was standing outside it with her three children. They all were huddled up together, looking nervous, like I was performing an exorcism on the other side of the door instead of taking a pregnancy test. Elaine was even biting her nails.

"I'm okay. I'm just waiting for the result."

"Did you pee on the right spot?" Elaine asked.

I didn't answer her because it was obvious I did. The damn line appeared on the stick. I threw the test and the results away. I washed my hands and walked out the bathroom.

"You goin' have a baby?" Brianna asked immediately.

I smiled at her and a tear slipped.

"Bri—you, Bryan, and Brandon go downstairs and finish watching TV," Elaine instructed her kids.

They reluctantly did what she had told them to, and Elaine followed me into the back room.

"It was positive?" Elaine asked as she closed the door behind her.

I sat down on the edge of the bed. I nodded. Then the tears came pouring. Elaine sat down beside me.

"Don't cry. It's going to be all right," she said as she rubbed my back. "It's not the end of the world, Angel. People have babies all the time. I know it seems hard to picture and I know it's scary right now, but you'll get through it."

Elaine wrapped her arms around me. She comforted me, and that made me cry more. I wished that she was my mom. I needed my mother desperately at that moment—and Elaine was nice and all, but I would have given anything to have been in my mother's arms rather than hers right then. But the phrase, *love the one you're with* came to my mind, and I opened my arms up and hugged Elaine back.

Elaine told me I could stay with her. She even told me not to worry about it when I promised her I would find a way to help her pay the bills. She said her only concerns were me getting back in school and making the right decisions about my pregnancy. At Elaine's house things were much different. I was eating three full-course meals a day. I was able to go right down in her basement and wash what little bit of clothes I had. She kept her house clean. She hardly had company. Matter of fact, the only person that ever came to the house since I'd been there was her kid's babysitter, Veronica, and she only came at night while Elaine worked the strip. The most important thing that had changed, though, was me. I hadn't smoked weed or taken Ecstasy since I got there. I felt good about that.

Especially for the sake of the baby that was growing inside me. I wasn't sure how far along I was, but Elaine had made me an appointment at a clinic to find out. It would be my first doctor's visit. It was scheduled for ten o'clock. I was on my way out the door at a quarter after nine. The kids had off from school due to the Christmas holiday so Elaine couldn't go with me to the doctor's because she had to stay home with them. I didn't mind though, because I had gotten in touch with my sister and my mom and they agreed to meet me there. I was so excited to see them after so long. Plus, my mom had been clean since she was in the shelter so she was in a different mind state when I talked to her and it made me feel good.

I got off the train and walked toward the clinic. In the distance I could see two people standing outside the building. One was a skinny woman smoking a cigarette and the other was a thick girl with a long ponytail.

"Naja!" I shouted as I got a little closer.

My little sister turned around and it looked like she had gained weight. She wasn't my little sister no more. Her breasts were bigger than mine and she had thighs and hips like a woman.

"Angel!" Naja called out as she jogged toward me.

We hugged each other tight for a while.

"I missed you, Angel! Where you been?" Naja whined.

"I missed you, too," I told her, walking the few feet to my mom.

"Heyyy," my mom said, taking one last puff from her cigarette and flicking it in the air.

I gave my mom a hug and looked her over. She put on a few pounds herself, but standing beside Naja, she looked thin.

"How you been?" she asked, smiling.

"All right," I told her, smiling back.

"So you done got pregnant?" she asked.

I grinned bashfully and nodded my head as I led my mom and Naja into the clinic.

"By Jamal?" Naja asked.

I nodded again.

"He asked about you, too," she said.

"For real? When? Where you see him at?"

"Mommy and me went around to the house to check the mail and see how much work the workers did to it, and he was walking out his house."

"What he say?"

"What, you don't talk to him no more?" my mom jumped back in.

"I ain't talk to him in a while. He mad at me."

"You done broke that boy heart?" my mom quizzed.

"He just was like, Where ya sister," Naja spoke over my mom. "I told him I ain't know."

"Why you tell 'im that?"

"That was before I got ya number from Aunt Jackie."

"Oh." Naja made my day, telling me that Jamal had asked about me. I figured I would go see him when we left the clinic.

We got in the waiting room and it was packed. *Jerry*

Springer was playing on a small TV that was hanging from the ceiling in a corner. My mom sat down in one of only four empty chairs. Naja joined me at the sign-in window.

"You have an appointment?" the receptionist asked.

"Yes."

She slid me a clipboard and a pen and said, "Sign in."

I scribbled my name, date, and time of appointment on the line and sat down. A few minutes later the receptionist called me back up to the window and asked if this was my first time there. I told her yeah, and she handed me some papers to fill out. Meanwhile Naja bombarded me with questions.

"So, how you find out you was pregnant? You keepin' it? Where was you staying at? You coming back home?"

She was probably just happy to see me. We chatted and put each other up on the latest. Then I was called to the back. The nurse said that one person was allowed to go back in the room with me. Naja thought it was going to be her, but my mom said she wanted to go back. I was surprised. My mom usually took the backseat when it came to me. She tended to be stand-offish. But that day she was playing her part. I was able to push any grudges I had held against her to the side.

Back in the room, a nurse took my blood pressure, weighed me, checked my heart rate, and recorded all this information in my file. Then she left my mom and me alone to wait for the doctor.

"So, are you nervous?" my mom asked.

"A little bit."

"I can't believe my baby is going to have a baby."

"I know. I can't believe it either."

"Did you plan it?"

I looked at my mom like she was crazy, and she explained herself, "What? Some girls your age be wanting to get pregnant. They be going through that little phase where they feel like they want somebody to love them and all that crap."

"Naw. Not me," I told her.

"So, do Jamal know? Why he ain't down here with you?"

"I told you I ain't talk to him in a while. I didn't even tell him yet."

"Well, girl, what you waitin' on?"

"I'ma tell him today if he home. I wanted to see how far I was and make sure everything was all right first."

"Oh, I heard you came by the shelter." My mom changed the subject. "I wanted to tell them to let you in, but they only had room for me and two kids. If I would have told them you was with us they would have made us leave. I felt so bad, though, but I figured you had somewhere to stay."

I thought that no matter what the explanation was, I would never forgive my mom for telling those people at the shelter that I wasn't her child, but when she explained the situation, it made sense—and I actually felt like I could forgive her.

"It's all right. I was mad when they told me, though. I thought you was just tellin' them that 'cause you was mad at me," I revealed.

"I wasn't mad at you. And even if I was, I wouldn't have done no shit like that. I know I did some fucked-up things while I was in my addiction, but you're my daughter. I wouldn't go that far."

"So you're clean now?" I asked my mom.

"Twenty-one days," she replied proudly.

"That's good," I told her.

"It sounds funny saying this, but it was a good thing going in the shelter. They got Kenny in preschool, and being away from Marvin plus having a curfew and stuff, I stopped doing dope."

"Yeah, Naja told me. She said they locked Marvin up."

"Yeah. He had warrants out on him and when they took him to the hospital the night of the fire they ran his name. Sure enough, they locked him up right after he got treated," my mom elaborated.

Although I was happy that Marvin had gotten arrested and was out of the picture, I didn't care to discuss him. "How is Kenny doin' in school?" I asked, switching the topic.

"He doin' all right. It took him a couple days to get used to it, but he's fine now. They give him homework and stuff. He be bringing me home pictures. He doin' good."

"All," I sighed. "I miss Kenny. Can I go by the shelter with y'all to see him?"

"Yeah, but you know, we're leaving the shelter. I gotta go past the house after this to see how far they got. They told me the house would be done by Christmas."

"Yeah, Naja told me the insurance company is paying for it."

"Yeah. I didn't even know we had it. But I was looking through some paperwork on the house and it showed that when Curtis paid off the house he paid the insurance up for five years."

"He's still taking care of us, ain't he," I spoke of my brother.

"I know. That's what I told Naja."

"Well, I'm glad everything is going good."

My mom was starting to say something, but there was a knock on the door.

"Hello," the doctor said, entering the room. "I'm Dr. Wise." She extended her hand to my mom first, then to me. We introduced ourselves to her.

"Your urinalysis made it clear that you are pregnant. Now, we just have to find out how far along you are," she began.

Then she asked me when was my last period. I told her the same thing I had told Elaine. From there, she instructed me to lie on my back and she put her fingers in my private and pressed down on my stomach. Based on my response about my period and her brief examination, she determined I was six and a half weeks and she gave me a due date of August 2. She asked me what were my plans as far as the baby was concerned. I told her that I planned on keeping it. Then she tuned to my mom and asked, "Are you the proud grandparent?"

"Yes."

"Well, make sure you stay on your daughter to follow up with checkups throughout her pregnancy and to take the prenatal vitamins I'm going to prescribe her," the doctor told my mom. "Getting prenatal care is the best first step pregnant woman can take."

My mom nodded in agreement. The doctor then told us that a nurse would be back in to give me some literature and the prescription as well as an appointment card to schedule my next visit. I got dressed, and after receiving the information from the nurse, my mom and I met Naja back in the waiting room.

"So what they say?" Naja asked all hype.

"I'm six and a half weeks."

"Oh, my God, I can't believe you having a baby. I hope it's a girl. I be seeing some cute clothes for girls. You can name her after me. Little Naja," my sister went on.

"Slow down," I told her. "You sound a little too excited about this baby. Let me be the one to tell you, it's nothing cute about me having a baby. I made a mistake."

"Thank you," my mom butted in.

"Whatever," Naja said.

My mom, Naja, and me went to Wendy's and ate lunch. Then we took the train to Brooklyn. We got to our block and it looked so festive. Christmas lights decorated the majority of the houses. There was even a car parked outside with MERRY X-MAS written in white shoe polish on the back window.

My mom's house looked a lot better than before. The windows were all in, and it looked like the roof had been replaced. My mom and Naja went inside to inspect it.

"You not comin' in?" my mom asked.

"I wanna see if Jamal home first," I said. "I'll look in there before I go."

"Well, if we ain't in here when you leave Jamal, meet us around Aunt Jackie house," my mom told me.

"All right," I said as I rang Jamal's doorbell and hoped he was home. I was anxious to see him.

"What's up?" Jamal asked, seemingly unenthused at my presence.

I didn't make a big deal out of his nonchalant attitude. It was my fault he felt whatever way he felt about me, so it was on me to work hard to change it.

"Can we talk?" I asked him in my sweetest tone of voice.

He opened the door wider for me to go in his house. He sat down on his sofa in his living room. I guessed he was giving me a hint that he expected our talk to be short by having me in his living room. We never sat in there. We either went in his room or in the basement. But again, the whole thing was my fault, so I was in no position to bitch about anything.

"What's up?" he repeated himself.

I sat down beside him and began, "First, I want to tell you I'm sorry."

He rolled his eyes and looked away as if he wasn't trying to hear anything I had to say.

"Jamal, believe me, I know that I hurt you. We had a good thing, and I fucked it up. I can't tell you how sorry I am. All I can do is show you."

"You know what you did, man? You sucked some nigga dick. That shit ain't forgivable. I could probably get past you workin' at a strip club and giving niggas lap dances and shit, but you put ya mouth on a nigga dick. A nigga you ain't even know. You let that nigga take pictures of you and every-thing. I wanted to fuck that pussy up when he showed us those pictures in the break room, but I couldn't 'cause then they would have known that you was my girl. You know how embarrassing that shit would've been? I had to sit there and look at them niggas go crazy over pictures of my girl sucking some nigga dick. Yo. You don't know how fucked up I felt— and still feel. The only reason you in here talking to me is 'cause I wanted you to know and understand how dirty you did me."

"I do know, and I do understand."

"I don't think you do. You come up here all cool and shit like it's nothin'."

"No, I didn't, Jamal. I know what I did was dirty, and I'm trying so hard to make you see that. I was high first of all, and second of all I was . . ."

Jamal cut me off. "What? You was getting high, too? What else was you doin' that I ain't know about? You was just a little freak on the side, huh? Stripping, getting' high, suckin' niggas' dicks. You was probably havin' threesomes, too, wasn't you?"

"Jamal, stop, please. I really don't want this to turn into no fight. I just want to explain myself."

"How? How can you explain that shit?"

I didn't know how to get through to Jamal. I was trying to make him understand my position, but it was damn near impossible. I couldn't blame him, though.

"I'm listening," he said.

"Jamal, you don't know what I been going through at home, and I was in a desperate situation," I started.

"I know what you was going through 'cause I was right there with you," Jamal whined.

"Yeah, you were. But, you don't know the half of it. It's a lot of stuff I didn't tell you."

"So, what that mean?"

"I'm not saying it means anything. I'm not trying to make excuses. You know me, and you know I would have never worked at no strip club if I didn't really need to. And as far as me getting high. I didn't do it voluntarily. They had put E-pills in my drink, and I didn't know it. I was out of character," I explained.

"I know you go through a lot with ya moms and dem. But you always was straight up with me about everything. You told me you was workin' at a hotel. I believed you. So it's not like I knew you was workin' at a strip club and then I saw the pictures. I was caught off guard all the way around. It was like you was playing me for a sucker the whole time."

"I know what it might seem like, but trust me, it wasn't like that at all. I didn't want you to know because I got a lot of love for you, Jamal. You are the only person I got, truthfully." I started to cry.

"That's why I don't understand how you could do me like that," he said as he, too, shed tears.

I reached over and wrapped my arms around him. We cried together and there was nothing I wanted more than to be able to console him. I loved him so much and I never meant to hurt him the way I did. I wanted to make it up to him so bad. I grabbed his face and kissed him on his lips. He returned the kiss reluctantly. I started rubbing him all over his body, and he was doing the same to me. I wanted him so bad and I was glad he let me have him.

Jamal unbuttoned his jeans and I sat on his lap from the back. He slid into me and we did it right there on the couch. When it was over, I cried again, but out of happiness. It seemed like I had rid myself of so much tension. Just to be in Jamal's arms again was fulfilling. I had missed him so much. He was all I needed. Nothing eased me like he did.

I had pulled my pants up, but left them opened. Then I cuddled up under Jamal. He was quiet like he was thinking about something. I didn't want bad memories to work him up again, so I figured I would get his mind on something else.

"Jamal, do you love me?"

"Yup," he said as if it hurt.

"I have something to tell you."

"What?" he asked defensively.

"I'm pregnant."

"Don't play like that, Angel."

"I'm not playing."

"That fast? Come on now."

"No. Not from just now. I'm six and a half weeks," I told him, pulling out the piece of paper I got from the doctor's.

Jamal took the paper and read it to himself.

"This is for real?" he asked.

"Um hum."

He was silent for a moment. Then he asked, "Is it mine?"

I was disappointed, but I guessed I had that coming. "Of

course. Look Jamal, I swear on my brother I didn't do it to nobody else. I know I messed up with you. But I'm not lying about this," I told Jamal, looking him in his eyes.

Jamal didn't say anything. He just placed my head back down on his chest. I took that as a good sign. I closed my eyes and said a silent prayer. I got my baby back, I thought, and as long as that was, nothing else in the world mattered.

✿

I wound up calling Elaine and telling her that I was going to stay at my mom's house over the holiday. She let me know that I was more than welcome to come back when-ever I needed to. I figured since my mom was getting herself together and her house was done and Marvin wasn't there and me and Jamal were on good terms, I would be all right staying back home. It wasn't until the day after Christmas that we were all able to actually move back in the house, though. We had stayed at Aunt Jackie's for the days before. We didn't have much of a Christmas. My mom was able to get a few toys for Kindle, and she got Naja two shirts and me a lotion and bubble bath set, but that was pretty much it. None of us complained though. We were just happy to be together, without Marvin. It felt like we were starting over fresh.

I hadn't been back to Elaine's, but I spoke to her on the phone almost every day since I been gone. I kept telling her I was going to go by her house and visit, but I had been spend-ing a lot of time with Jamal, so I kept putting it off. Me and him were slowly working things out. We had our ups and downs. Every so often, he would catch feelings about what I did and we would get into it. But for the most part, he was trying to forgive me. And being pregnant counted for something because he was trying extra hard to make it work for the baby.

It was the Monday after New Year's and I had a doctor's appointment. Jamal had taken off of work to go with me. I had my first ultrasound. Jamal's face lit up when the doctor let us hear the baby's heartbeat and watch it go up and down on the monitor. He looked at the pictures, which looked like nothing but darkness with specks of white space, the whole ride home. He was happy. It was January 2, and I remembered that Cat and Stacey said they would be back to work on that day so I told Jamal that when we got around our way, I wanted to stop by their store. I had so much to tell Stacey, and I knew she would have stories for me, too. Plus, I missed them two and couldn't wait to see them.

Jamal and me got off the bus right in front of C&S's. The door was open, but the gates were still pulled down over the window. Inside, there was an unfamiliar man sweeping the floor.

"I'm sorry, we're closed," the man said with a heavy Jamaican accent.

"Oh," I said. "Do you know when Cat and Stacey are coming back?"

The man stopped sweeping and looked at me. "Do you know them?"

"Yeah. I'm good friends with them," I told him with a smile

on my face. "I know they were in Jamaica, but I thought they would be back by now."

"Yeah, well, I'm sorry to tell you tis but, Stacey and my brudda Cat were killed in a plane crash yesterday." Tears gathered in the man's eyes.

"Huh?" I asked, hoping I heard him wrong.

He bowed his head and said, "I'm sorry."

I put my hand on my chest. I couldn't believe what I had heard. I grew speechless. Jamal stepped in and asked the man about funeral arrangements. But I hardly heard what was being said. I was in a state of shock. I wanted to break down and cry, but nothing came out. I was numb. I couldn't and I wasn't trying to register the information. That couldn't have been true, I thought. God wouldn't have done that to me.

Home Is Where the Heart Is

My mom, Jamal, and me were walking up the block on our way to C&S's. Cat and Stacey's family planned a memorial for them in front of the store since they had their funerals in Jamaica. It was cold outside. I remember the weatherman saying it was only going to be twenty-three degrees and the wind making it feel like eighteen. He ain't never lied, I thought as the wind whipped my face.

When we got to the store there was a crowd of people out there. Most were people we knew from the neighborhood. A few were Cat and Stacey's family members, and there were a couple people out there I never saw before. On an easel was a blow-up picture of Cat and Stacey, and on the ground, surrounding it, were stuffed animals and flowers. I walked up and placed a rose and a sandwich bag with two dollars' worth of quarters in it among the memorabilia. I took a moment to look at the items and then at the picture. I couldn't believe that was happening—I was at a memorial for my two favorite people in the world.

Walking back to where I had been standing with my mom and Jamal, I started crying. I didn't know what I was going to do without that store and without Stacey and Cat. Thinking about it made my heart ache, and then imagining how they died made it worse. I felt for them. I cried so hard I couldn't stop. Jamal held me in his arms and my mom rubbed my back, but I didn't feel any better. I did not want to feel that pain. It was too much for me. I wanted so bad to go smoke a blunt.

Cat's brother, the man who told us about the plane crash, started off the memorial with the Lord's Prayer. Some people recited the words with him, others, like myself, were crying and whimpering. After the prayer, a woman stepped from out the crowd to read a poem she had written. It described how Cat and Stacey touched her life. I wished I could write, because I would have written a poem for them, too. They had done so much for me, just them being there and letting me sit in their store for hours helped me so much. I was truly going to miss them. Another lady from the crowd read a poem, and then Cat's brother asked that we have a moment of silence. Everybody bowed their heads. People quieted their cries, but not me. I couldn't help it. I didn't want to disturb the moment of silence, so I just walked away for a minute.

Jamal followed me a couple stores down. He wrapped his

arms around me and rocked me back and forth. At the least, I was thankful he was there. There would have been no way I would have got through that by myself.

"It's all right," Jamal whispered. "They're in peace, now, watching over you."

I wiped my face and looked up at Jamal. "That's bullshit," I told him, angrily.

Before he could say anything, it started to snow. Out of nowhere snowflakes were falling from the dark sky. Jamal looked at me and said, "It's not bullshit." He picked a snowflake off my nose. "See, that's God."

I put my head back on Jamal's chest and tried to feel what he said. But it was hard. Just like it was when I lost my brother.

"I just want to say thank you all for coming out here and taking part in this with us," I heard Cat's brother say.

People started walking away, going back to their lives. Cat's brother took the picture of Cat and Stacey down and put it in the back of a minivan. My mom started to walk toward Jamal and me. Her face was twisted up. "That's a damn shame," she said to us.

And that was it. Cat and Stacey were gone. They were just memories. That shit hurt.

❀

I been back home for a couple months and things were better. My mom was going to N.A. meetings every week and she took Naja and me to a few. Hearing the other people's stories, I understood more about addiction and the crazy, some-times cruel, things it made people do. I realized that no mat-ter how bad I had it, there was someone somewhere who had it worse. With that, I was able to forgive my mom for the things she had done in the past and move on. I just hoped she stayed clean. I, myself, was taking advantage of having a functional household again. I did some research to find out how I could get back in school and all I had to do was take a test. The test would determine what grade they would put me in. I was scheduled to take it in a week after I enrolled in my neighborhood school. Of course I wasn't able to go back to my old school, but school was school no matter where it was. I just wanted to finish ninth grade.

I woke up one morning and I didn't feel sick. I went to the bathroom to pee. Naja and Kindle were both in school. I went downstairs, and *The Price Is Right* was on TV, but nobody was in the living room watching it so I turned it off. My mom was in the kitchen cleaning.

"Why you turn my TV off?" my mom asked as soon as I entered the kitchen.

" 'Cause wasn't nobody in there watching it. That's wastin' electricity," I told her.

"You worrying about the electric bill like you pay it," my mom said, wiping the inside of the refrigerator.

"You should be happy. I'm tryin' to save you money."

"Child, please. Aunt Jackie hooked me up with one of Hasaan's friends, and he turned the electric on for free. I don't gotta pay no monthly bill no more," my mom bragged.

"Oh, well, in that case," I said as I walked in the living room and turned *The Price Is Right* back on.

"What you cleaning all crazy for? We having an inspection or something?" I asked, grabbing a box of cereal out the cabinet.

"It's spring cleaning time," my mom answered.

"Oh." I got out a bowl and a spoon and poured me some cereal. "Mom, pass me the milk out of there."

My mom paused her scrubbing and handed me the carton of milk.

"You must not have morning sickness, you drinking milk."

"No. I feel fine today, thank goodness. I think it's because I'm in my second trimester now."

"Well, good. You can go to the Laundromat," my mom assigned me a duty. "I have a couple loads for me and Kindle. You can get you and Naja's stuff together. Just don't go over five loads. That's all I got enough for until next week."

"Why? What happened to your money? Didn't you just get ya stamps?" I asked, overprotective of my mom's spending. I was concerned she might have relapsed.

"Yeah. But I bought food. Plus, I lent Aunt Jackie some money to pay her rent. She goin' pay me back when she get her money next week."

"Don't Aunt Jackie get Section Eight?" I inquired further.

"Yeah, they pay most of her rent, but she still gotta pay two hundred out her pocket."

"A three-bedroom house for two hundred a month, I wish."

"I'm tellin' you. I wish I could get Section Eight, shit, I

would get another house. Let them give me Section Eight, I'll get a vacation home down on the beach like in Wildwood or something, rent that bad boy out for like a thousand dollars a month, give the landlord the little hundred to two hundred and keep the other eight or nine for myself. I could get rich off that shit."

"Dat's a good plan. How you get on Section Eight?"

"It's a bunch of bullshit involved. You gotta be homeless just to get on the waiting list."

"Oh." I finished my bowl of cereal and got dressed to go to the Laundromat. I wanted to go as early as possible before it got crowded. I gathered up Naja's bag of dirty clothes and the few outfits I had and put them in the trash bag with my mom and Kindle's stuff. I put the bag in the cart along with the soap powder and bleach. Then I dragged it out the door and down the steps. The weather was nice compared to the cold snowy days we had in January and most of February. It felt like that early March cold where you needed a coat but not a hat and scarf.

I walked up to Newton's. It was a few people in there, but there were plenty of washers available, which was why I went early. I put the white clothes in first, and as I was putting the darks in something told me to check the pockets to my jeans. Inside one I found a business card. It had information about an outreach program on it. Then a vague image of the man who gave it to me popped in my head. I held on to the business card and planned to call the number later, but I was bored waiting for the clothes to wash so I fulfilled my curiosity and called from the pay phone in the Laundromat.

"Hello, Street to Runway, how may I direct your call?" the professional woman's voice greeted me.

"Hello, may I speak to a . . . Ron Washington?" I hesitated because it was funny how the man had the same last name as me.

"May I ask who's calling?"

"Angel Washington," I answered.

"Please hold."

The woman must have thought I was related to the man because she didn't ask the other question that usually followed "Who's calling?" which was "What's this is in reference to?"

"Hello, this is Ron," the man said when he picked up.

"Hi, I'm Angel Washington, I got your card a while ago and I wanted to know more about your program."

"Well, Ms. Washington, first, let me ask you this, is your grandmother's name Edith?"

"No," I replied reluctantly, not knowing the relevance of his question.

"Oh, well I guess we're not related," he joked.

I chuckled at his not-so-funny humor.

"I'm just joking. I'm in a good mood today. But anyway, Streets to Runway is a nonprofit organization I started to help get women runaways, prostitutes, and drug addicts off the streets and back into society as functioning and productive citizens," he explained. "It's a modeling agency that caters to outreach programs. For example, our women are called on to host community events, assist at job and health fairs, and speak at schools, prisons, detention centers, rehabs, etcetera."

"Oh, okay," I said.

"Do you mind telling me where you got my card from?"

"A friend of mine gave it to me," I lied.

"Oh, well, if you're interested in seeing what we're about, please come down to the office. You can drop in any day of the week between nine and one and then again between two and five. We will gladly give you or your friend more information. Okay?"

"Okay, thanks."

"Oh, and the address should be on the card. We're in Harlem."

"Okay. Thank you," I said.

"Thank you. Bye now."

I hung up the phone and was intrigued. I was interested in finding out more. I made a mental note to go down to the office that next day. I figured I would see about getting a job there, maybe something part time just to have a little bit of money to help my mom out and to save up for the baby.

It took about three and a half hours to wash and dry the five loads. I went home and called Elaine.

"Well, hello," Elaine sang.

"Hi, Elaine," I sang back.

"How are you?"

"I'm doing good. What about you?"

"I'm hangin' in there."

"Listen," I said. "I want you to go somewhere with me tomorrow."

"Where?"

"It's right in Harlem. Not too far from you. It's a modeling agency."

"You wanna model?" Elaine grew excited.

"Well, not really like model like magazines and fashion shows, but like speaking to kids and helping people out and stuff."

"Oh, okay. Well, what time do you want to go? I have to take the kids to school at seven thirty. So any time after that will be fine."

"We can go from nine to one or two to five. I was thinking being there at like ten. You know I like to handle all my business early to beat the traffic."

"You and me both. Well, okay. That's a plan. How's your mom doing?"

"She's doing good. She's still going to meetings and stuff, so . . ."

"Good, good. Well, I'm glad you called me, but my stories are on, so call me in the morning okay?"

"Oh, okay. No problem. Talk to you tomorrow."

"Bye-bye."

I borrowed a black blouse from my mom, ironed it, and hung it up. I laid my jeans across the banister in the hall. I was ready for the trip to the agency. I felt good about it.

Knock! Knock! The bang on my bedroom wall woke me up. I reached down to the floor and placed my hand on the phone. It rang almost instantly.

"I'm up," I answered on the first ring.

"What time you have to be down there?" Jamal asked.

"I'm trying to be there by ten."

"Well, my mom said I can hold her car. I'll take you."

"You don't have to. I know you have to go to work."

"I got a little bit of time to spare. If I get you down there at ten I can be back up here by like eleven. That's enough time for me to get to work by twelve."

"Aww, Jamal, I appreciate it."

Jamal avoided the mushiness and said, "So you can lay back down and get you some more sleep. I'll wake you up in a hour."

"Thank you, baby."

"Uh-huh," he said.

Jamal loved me so much but it was obvious sometimes that since I messed up and cheated on him he was holding back.

The extra hour I had to sleep went by so fast it might as well have been five minutes. I got up and got dressed. My mom was still asleep when I left out the house. I left her a note explaining where I was going and what time I expected to be back.

I called Elaine from Jamal's cell phone and told her I was on my way to the place. She said to call her when I was like five minutes away and she would leave her house and get in a cab.

"Elaine, I'm about five minutes away," I told her when the time came.

"Okay. I'll see you there."

"Now where do you know her from again?" Jamal asked. He had become so inquisitive.

"I met her through Antione. They used to work together, and when he got locked up he asked her if I could stay with her," I said, making sure I repeated the exact answer I had given him the first time he asked me where I knew Elaine from.

I kept a lot from Jamal, and not out of being sneaky or nothing. It was just that it was too sensitive a time to tell him about me getting locked up and having to stay with Butter and meeting Elaine on a damn hooker strip. That would have ended our relationship for sure, and I didn't want that. Besides, Jamal didn't need to know all that, because it had nothing to do with where we were at that point. It was irrelevant.

"Thank you so much, boo," I told Jamal as I leaned over and kissed him on his cheek.

"Um hum," he mumbled.

I got out of the car and walked up to the building with the address that matched that on the business card.

"Good luck," Jamal said out the window.

I smiled at him and went inside. I waited a couple minutes for Elaine. We greeted each other with a hug when she got there and then took the elevator to the seventh floor.

"Good morning, ladies," a tall, dark-skinned lady said to us when we walked through the office door.

"Good morning," Elaine said.

"Hello," I said.

The woman looked at Elaine with wide eyes, as if she was waiting for her to tell her what she was there for. Elaine stepped to the side and pointed to me. "I'm just here with her," she said.

"Oh. What brings you in today?" the woman asked.

"I spoke with Ron Washington yesterday and he told me I could come down here and get more information about the program."

"Oh, okay. You're Angel Washington?" she quizzed, glancing down at some scribbled notes on her desk.

"Yes."

"Oh, okay. I'm Margie. It's nice to meet you. Have a seat, and I'll call Mr. Washington for you."

"She is so polite," I whispered to Elaine as we sat down in the chairs a few feet away from Margie's desk.

Waiting for Mr. Washington, I looked around the office. There were pictures hanging up of women in groups, at speaking engagements, and at fairs. In between the pictures were framed quotes that said things like ONE STEP AND WILLPOWER CAN GET YOU THROUGH A DAY. ONE DREAM AND DETERMINATION CAN GET YOU THROUGH LIFE. A good feeling came over me. I hoped the place was everything I had imagined it would be, and most important I hoped they were hiring and I qualified.

A few minutes went by and Mr. Washington came into the waiting area and invited Elaine and me into his office. He looked at me strangely, like he recognized me, but he didn't say anything. I guessed he figured I didn't want to discuss how we met since I had lied and told him I got his card from a friend. Inside his office, he explained the organization in detail for Elaine and then answered our questions. He gave us some literature to take with us and then took us on a tour of the building. He told us they were always hiring because their mission was to get as many women off the streets as possible so they never turned anyone away. The only thing was there was a process you had to go through before officially being one of their employees. An application, a criminal background check, and a drug test were the major components. I was cool with everything but the background check. I wasn't sure if they had put a warrant out on me since I never went to my court hearing and I didn't want Mr. Washington to find out and turn me in.

"I knew it was too good to be true," I told Elaine as we waited for the elevator.

"Why do you say that?"

"They do background checks and I might have a warrant out on me," I revealed.

"For what? Oh goodness, girl. You come fully loaded, don't you?"

"No, it's nothing like that. When they raided Shake's they locked me up for being underage. That's all. I just never went to court for it."

"Oh. That's nothing, and anyway, the way Mr. Washington was talking, he can help you clear that up. He said they didn't mind criminal records because of the type of women they hired. He just said that you couldn't have any open cases without addressing them. So, shucks, you might wanna let him look you up. For one, he can tell you if you even have a warrant and two, he can help you clear it up," Elaine said, shedding light on the situation.

"That's true," I said. "Well, I'll probably fill out everything and bring it back down here. I wouldn't mind working at a place like this." We got in the elevator.

"Yeah. It's nice. The people are nice," Elaine commented.

"You should work here, too," I said, getting to the point of why I asked Elaine to go with me in the first place.

"Oh no, not me. The pay isn't enough for a woman with three kids. Now for you, it's fine. You're young, you stay at home with your mom, and you'll only have one baby."

"Well, you should think about it. It's better than working the strip."

Elaine frowned at me and said, "Oh, Angel, don't go there. I've been doing what I do for long enough to know my options, trust me. I know what I'm doing. I'm a grown woman."

"I didn't mean to offend you. I was just speaking out of concern." I said, trying to clear things up.

"It's okay. I know you didn't mean anything by it. But you don't have to be concerned about me, sweetie. You have so much to worry about as it is. I appreciate it though—but I know what I'm doing."

Elaine gave me a hug and got in a cab to go home. I thanked her for going with me and apologized again for the comment I made. I truly didn't mean to offend her, and I felt bad that I did because she had been nothing but nice to me.

I took the train back to Brooklyn. I walked pass C&S's. It was clear that the weather and time had discolored the stuffed animals and killed the flowers, but they were still there. Even the bag of quarters I left was intact. That just showed how much love and respect people had for Cat and

Stacey. Not even a smoker resorted to stealing the change. I walked down my block, skimming over the application I had. My mind immediately started mapping out a plan. I would get the job at the agency, pass ninth grade, and then by the time I would have the baby I'd have a little stash and could chill for a little while then start tenth grade like in October. My mom could watch the baby while I went to school and the money I got from welfare to pay for day care I could use to help my mom out and buy the baby some stuff.

I got to my front door and turned the key. I walked in my house and almost fainted.

"Hey, Angel," Marvin said with a smile on his face.

I stared right through him, disgusted at his presence. I didn't speak to him out of shock, fear, and anger. *Where is my mom,* I thought. *She better not be planning on letting him stay here. How the hell did his ass get out of jail? And why is he back in my house?*

"Hey Angel, how did it go at the job interview?" my mom asked, walking downstairs.

I looked at her suspiciously, my eyes roaming to her arms, her eyes, and her balance. I wondered if she had been up in the bathroom getting high. With Marvin sitting there, you never knew what was going on. He was bad people, and wherever he was a storm was sure to follow.

"It was all right," I said out the corner of my mouth.

"Oh. They let Marvin out," she said joyously.

"Um," I huffed and walked up to my room.

I slammed the door and put the lock on it. I didn't want him coming nowhere near me, especially while I was carrying a baby. I wanted to go downstairs and ask my mom had she lost her mind and remind her that she said being away from Marvin helped her stop shooting up. So what did she think was going to happen now that he was back, I wondered. Did she think she would stay clean and be with him at the same time? If she did, she was dumber than I thought, and I was giving her one day to see if she would let him stay. If so, I was out of there. I didn't care where I went and even though my home was where my heart was, with Marvin in there, it was where my hell was—and I wanted no more parts of hell.

Same Shit, Different Toilet

"No! No! Please, Marvin! Stop!" I yelled, holding on to the banister that led down to the basement.

"You want ya mother to hear you?" Marvin asked. "Keep on yellin' like that and I'ma beat that baby out of you."

Marvin was pulling me, trying to get me down the steps. This was the first time since he had been back at our house that he had tried this with me, and it had been a few weeks. I thought that it was because I was pregnant, but I was wrong. I was showing and everything and that didn't matter to him that morning. But it mattered to me. I never used to put up a fight with Marvin because he always threatened me. But even with the threats of him beating my baby out of me, I was fighting back. I would have rather him do that then put his nasty, dirty dick anywhere near my child.

"No! Stop!" I continued to yell. All I wanted to do was eat my cereal in peace, I thought while I was holding on to the banister with all the strength I had.

Marvin's eyes were bloodshot red and veins started to pop out of his neck. He gritted his teeth like a pit bull and said, "You're playin' games with me?!" Then he took one of his hands off me and slapped me across my face.

The slap caught me off guard and made me lose my grip on the banister. I stumbled and almost fell on Marvin and down the steps.

"Aaarh!" I screamed as Marvin dragged me down the basement steps.

"You done pissed me off, now!" he said, standing over me, practically ripping off his pants.

At that point I was outraged and in so much pain. I didn't care if he beat me to death, I was going to fight him. I grabbed his wobbling calves to lift myself up, at that same time making him fall over. I got up off the floor and tried to run up the stairs. I thought I had it, but right as I reached my hand out to push open the basement door, I felt Marvin's hand wrap tightly around my ankle.

I used my hands to keep my face from hitting the steps as Marvin pulled me down them.

"Marvin, please," I begged, my eyes filled with tears. I was out of breath and weak. I couldn't fight back anymore if I wanted to, and at that point I wasn't sure I wanted to. I knew I had said I didn't care if he beat me to death, but that was because I didn't think he would. But I realized that he just might. So I tried to get him to stop civilly. I tried to buy some time and I hoped and prayed that in that time he would come down from his high and let me go. He didn't. I cried and begged the whole time from beginning to end. I damn near lost my voice. But he kept going until he was finished. Then he rolled off of me and laid on the cold basement floor in satisfaction. I got up slowly, pulled my pants and panties up, and limped up the steps. I walked past the bowl of cereal that I had been eating before Marvin came into the kitchen. And I walked out the front door.

Knock! Knock! Knock! I banged on Jamal's door.

"What happened?" Jamal asked, concerned.

I could barely talk. I was so sore and I couldn't stop crying.

"Jamal, I need to go to the hospital," I managed to say. "I think I'm bleeding."

Before Jamal could say anything, his mom was standing behind him.

"What she want this time of the morning?" she asked.

"Mom, it's not the time."

"My stomach is hurting, Jamal," I said, bent over, still at his doorway.

Jamal helped me inside his house.

"What happened?" he repeated.

"My stomach," I said.

"What are you bringing your stomach pains over here for? Don't no doctors live over here," Jamal's mom said.

"Mom! She's pregnant, all right! It's not the time!" Jamal snapped.

"Pregnant!" she shouted, "By who?"

I lifted my head up and looked at Jamal's mom.

"Ms. Brenda, I'm pregnant by Jamal, and I'm in a lot of pain, so . . ."

She cut me off, "Excuse me? You a stripper, you cheated on my son, disappeared, and come back talkin' about you pregnant with his baby! And you think I'm just goin' buy that!"

"Mom! Yo! Chill out!" Jamal defended me.

"Yes. Please, because I need to get to a hospital," I said, talking back to Jamal's mom for the first time.

Her face lit up. She was on fire, I could tell. But I didn't care. I just needed Jamal to take me to the hospital. I was scared for my baby, and his mom wasn't making matters no better.

"Oh no, you didn't!" she shouted. "Yes, please me in my house! You must have lost ya mind! You have got to go, okay! Out of my house! My son ain't claimin' no babies unless a paternity test says it's his! Ya word is as good as those bruises on ya face—very questionable!"

I looked at Jamal, then at his mom, and I realized I had no win. Jamal had eventually taken his mom's side. I could tell that he had taken what she said to heart. He was probably starting to question my baby being his. That was why he didn't say anything in my defense anymore. I knew what it was, so I just left. Jamal didn't come after me. He didn't offer to call me an ambulance, nothing. His mom had got in his head with that comment. I couldn't blame him, though. I got myself in that situation, so I had to get myself out.

I walked up my street, holding my stomach. The guy that lived in the crack house was on his porch.

"You all right?" he asked me.

I didn't want to, but I started crying. I shook my head.

"Yo, you need a doctor or somethin'?"

I nodded.

He ran off his porch and helped me up the steps and then into his house. He sat me on his sofa.

"I'ma call the ambulance for you, okay?" he said, heading for his kitchen.

I nodded again. I was in so much pain. I leaned my head on the arm of the couch and closed my eyes. I heard him on the phone with the ambulance. Then I heard somebody walking down his steps. I opened my eyes.

"Ant Man? What you doin' here?" I asked, tears still falling down my face.

"I'm servin'. What you doin' here is the question?" he asked. "You okay?"

"My stomach hurtin'," I told him.

He looked at me closely. "You pregnant?"

"Yeah, and I think something is wrong."

Just then the guy came out of the kitchen. "The ambulance is on they way."

"Naw, it's cool. She don't need 'em. I'll take her to the hospital."

"Word?"

"Yeah."

"That's okay with you, shorty?"

I nodded as I slowly lifted myself off the couch.

"She my peoples," Antione told the guy.

"Oh, damn, I ain't know that. It's a small world, ain't it."

Antione helped me out the house and into the backseat of a car that was parked outside. Some other guy was already in the driver seat. He looked at me strangely. He probably thought I was a crack-head. I was sure I looked like one, all sweated out and bruised, coming out of a crack house. Then he shot Antione a look like he wanted to say *What the hell you bring this pregnant crack-head in my car for?*

"This my peoples. Take her up the way," Antione instructed the driver before he had the chance to ask anything.

The guy huffed, put the car in drive, and pulled out of the parking space.

I was in a lot of pain and didn't feel like talking, but I was curious about when Antione had got out of jail.

"When did you get out?"

"Get out of where?"

"Wasn't you locked up?"

"Naw."

"Butter told me you got locked up out of town around the time they ran in Shake's," I explained.

"Ohhh. Naw. I was out of town. The cops ran up in my crib but it wasn't shit there. Naw, I ain't get locked up."

I left it at that. I wasn't in the mood to interrogate him anyway. Shit, what was done was done. I wasn't going to cry over spilled milk. Besides, I shouldn't have trusted Butter's word. I should have went by Antione's house myself. That was my fault.

Antione took a dutch from behind his ear and lit it. He took a few puffs on it and passed it to the driver. The smell was tempting. It reminded me of how good I felt whenever I smoked weed. I was in so much pain, physically and emotionally, and I wanted something that would make it go away. That blunt was calling me.

"Ant man, can you pass that back here please?"

"But you pregnant."

"I know, but it hurts so bad. Just a little bit to take my mind off this pain," I whined.

Antione took another puff and then passed it back to me. When I got the dutch in my hand, I hesitated. I thought about the baby, but something inside me told me that my baby was already harmed. It told me I might as well go ahead and smoke it. I puffed it. Then I puffed it again and again and again. After a while I laid my head back and just chilled out.

"I thought up the way was the hospital," I snapped when I realized Antione and the guy had driven me to Butter's house.

"Angel, you can't go to no hospital after you done smoked weed while you pregnant. They ain't goin' do nothin' but run ya name, see that you got a warrant, lock you up, and take ya baby from you the minute it's born."

He made sense, but why Butter's house? Why not his own? I was steamed, but I wasn't stupid. Something wasn't right with that picture. Then Butter came out of her house. She approached the passenger door and bent over like she was going to kiss Antione, but Antione stopped her.

"Look who I ran into," he said.

Butter looked in the back seat. The expression on her face when she saw me was unforgettable.

"What corner you pick that ho up from?" she asked.

"Be nice," Antione said. "She pregnant and shit."

"She knocked up?" Butter asked with an attitude. "What kind of money is she goin' make knocked up?"

"Pregnant pussy is the best pussy," Antione replied. "You ain't know that."

I started to put the pieces together in my head, and I knew what was wrong with the picture. I was surrounded by a bunch of shady bastards who had a fucked-up scheme going on and were trying to involve me in it.

"Ant man, I don't care about the police locking me up. I just wanna make sure my baby is all right," I told Antione, with hopes he would have a heart and take me to the hospital.

Instead, Antione got out of the car and opened the back door. He grabbed me by my arm and pulled me out. I looked at him with so much anger and hate. I hoped he would get the picture and realize that he was dead wrong for whatever he was about to do. He just smirked. Butter walked up the steps to her brownstone and opened the door. Antione forcefully pushed me in the house. The driver took off.

Once I was inside Butter's house, I thought about giving up. I didn't say anything. I didn't put up a fight. My stomach pains were coming back, and honestly, I just wanted to die. I was asking myself, how did that morning go from me getting up, getting dressed, eating, and getting ready to go take the test to get me back in school, to me being raped, cussed out by Jamal's mom, and then brought here to Butter's house for more abuse by Antione, my own fuckin' family.

"You look like you need a bath," Butter said with her lips twisted up.

"Yo, clean 'er up, get 'er some weed, and let 'er chill," Antione told Butter.

Butter rolled her eyes at me and walked up the stairs. That was the first time I seen Butter actually take orders from somebody. She didn't even listen to Shake like that. Meanwhile, Antione pulled me over to the couch and sat me down.

I figured that was a perfect opportunity to find out what was going on with him and see if I could snap him out of his obvious insanity.

"Ant Man," I shouted, "What is up with you? Why are you doin' this to me? It's me. Curt's sister. Me and you are like family. What are you doin'?"

"Go upstairs and get cleaned up," he said, ignoring all of what I said.

He pulled some money from his pocket and started counting it. He didn't seem to have any remorse for my situation. He knew that I was in pain. He knew that I was pregnant and needed to go to a hospital, but it didn't seem to matter to him. Me being his little sister went out of the window. I didn't even know the nigga that was sitting there in Butter's living room counting a fistful of fifties. He sure wasn't the Antione I grew up with. He was no different than Butter and probably worse. I was disgusted at him and her, and I would kill them both if I had the chance.

"Go 'head," Antione reiterated about me going upstairs and taking a bath.

I slowly walked up the steps and into the back bedroom that was once mine. I sat down on the bed and cried. In no time, Butter came into the room with a blunt. She took a puff and gave it to me. She put an ashtray on the floor in front of me and left the room, closing the door behind her.

I put the blunt in the ashtray. I wasn't smoking shit from her. I didn't care how bad I wanted to. I heard somebody walk up the steps and down the hall. Then I heard Antione's voice. It was muffled, like he was whispering. I heard Butter whispering back. They sounded like they were in the bath-room next to the room I was in. I got up and put my ear to the door.

"Go a little easy on 'er," Antione whispered.

"Since when you want me goin' easy on a ho?"

"Don't get it confused, ain't nothin' changed around here. It's just that I feel a little bad for her. I was part of the reason her brother got killed, the least I can do is cut 'er some slack in this muthafucka."

"All right," Butter stretched her words with attitude.

I walked out into the hall. I was ready to fight a mother-fucker. "Antione, what the fuck did you just say?"

Butter looked like she was going to hit me, and I ain't give a fuck. I was ready for her 'cause her ass whippin' was long overdue. But Antione intercepted her.

"I got this," he said as he grabbed my arm and walked me

back in the room. He closed the door behind him, leaving Butter out in the hall.

"Antione, I don't believe you! It was you who got Curtis killed? You was like his fuckin' brother! He looked out for you! Why the fuck would you do something like that to him?"

Antione's face grew angrier. "It's so much more to the story, you don't even know. Ya mom set that up. I just didn't stop it!"

"Stop with ya bullshit! You did enough, okay! You hurt me enough!" I screamed, picking the blunt up out of the ashtray.

"No! You wanna be in grown folks' business, then you goin' listen!" Antione said. "Ya mom had a problem way before Curt died. She owed so many people so much money from gambling. And Curtis would pay niggas off for her over and over again. And the more he made, the more she gambled and the more she owed. Then Curtis told her he wasn't payin' no more niggas for her. He told her she needed to stop with the gambling and the drinking and get her shit together. She begged him to pay one last debt and he was like naw. And I ain't blame 'im either, 'cause she was takin' advantage of 'im."

In between taking puffs off the blunt, I cut Antione off. "She ain't have my brother killed! I don't care what you say. She might have had a gambling problem, she might have drank, but I know my mom and she do a lot of fucked-up shit, but she ain't have my brother killed. Curtis was my mom's heart!"

"She ain't have him killed. She had 'im robbed. But the robbery turned into a homicide. She ain't mean for him to be killed. She just told the dudes she owed money to where they could collect it from. She knew he was going to sell a beat. She knew he was going to have money on 'im. I'm the one who told her our route."

"So both of y'all bastards set my brother up?!"

"Ya mom owed me money. Matter fact to this day she owe me money! I wanted to get paid. The other niggas she owed wanted to get paid. And all Curt had to do was give up the money. I told 'im to give it up and we'd see those niggas later. But he wanted to be hardheaded and hit the gas. None of that shit would have went down if he would have just gave them niggas what they was askin' for. They ain't have no intentions on killin' nobody. That wasn't the plan. But y'all some hard-headed mothafuckas. You and ya brother both. See all this shit you goin' through right now. Had you just fuckin' stayed here at Butter's house, did what you was told, I would have been paid off and you wouldn't be here right now, chokin' on ya own tears and shit! Lookin' fuckin' pathetic!"

"Antione, I don't believe you!" I cried. "My mom and my brother looked out for you! When ya mom died, my mom took you in our house! She fed ya ass, she clothed ya ass, she made sure you was taken care of!"

"She ain't do shit! She was always talkin' about she couldn't afford to take care of me and she was ready to let the city come and get me! She ain't start actin' like she cared until I started hustlin' and helpin' her pay niggas off. That's when she was like call me Mom! She shady, Angel! And she usin' you to pay off her debts just like she used Curt! And you know what she owe me? Fourteen thousand! You ain't worth but fourteen thousand to ya mom."

"Aaaarrrh! Aaaarrrh!" I screamed.

I thought smoking would ease the pain, but it only got worse. I dropped the blunt back in the ashtray, and I grabbed my stomach with my other hand. I felt like I was going to faint. My heart was racing and another sharp pain shot through my stomach.

"Ouuuuch! Oh, my Godddd!"

Butter walked in the room. "Antione, what the hell is goin' on in here?"

Antione shook his head. "This little bitch don't have a clue. She done got herself in some shit she don't know how to get out of."

Butter turned to me. "I know you don't think you havin' that baby in my house!"

"I don't know what the fuck she doin'," Antione said, carelessly.

"You know what, Antione, enough is enough. Fuck her! Get her out of here! It ain't even worth it no more. I don't need no heat brought to my house. This could jeopardize everything."

"She goin' make my money," Antione insisted.

"Oh Godddd hellllp me!" I screamed. I was starting to breathe heavy. I was feeling dizzy. And the pain was excruciating. I tried to stand up, but my legs felt too heavy. I tried to use the wall to lift me off the bed.

"Money? How? Where? She is about to have a baby, Antione! And it's a strong possibility that it'll die in here. We don't need no dead babies in this house. The cops'll be all through here and for what? A grudge? You take that up with her mother at another time. Right now, you need to get her out of here."

Antione took heed to what Butter told him. He put his arms under mine and dragged me out the room and down the steps.

I was in so much pain physically and emotionally and I could hardly talk, but I managed to tell Antione, "I swear on my brother's grave, if I had a gun I would kill you."

When It Rains, It Pours

Antione left me out on the corner. I was leaned against a mailbox when a cab pulled over to let people out. It was a man and a woman, and when they saw me in the condition I was in they put me in the cab and told the driver to take me to a hospital. I didn't want him to do that because of what Antione had told me about them locking me up. But I was in too much pain to argue with the people or the cabdriver. We pulled up to the Metropolitan Hospital Center in Manhattan. The cabdriver flagged down a doctor, and I was put in a wheelchair and rushed to a room. My clothes were stripped off, an IV was put in my vein, and after eleven hours of labor pains, I had my son prematurely. He only weighed a pound. He was pale yellow and tiny like a kitten. They had to hook him up to all kinds of machines immediately after he was born. I didn't even get to hold him. They just let me glance at him, and they whisked him away. I was hurt by it at first, but it was for his safety. The doctors explained that he wasn't able to breathe and swallow on his own and his organs weren't fully developed, so he had to be watched closely. I couldn't argue with that.

Between the doctors giving me so many drugs and me having a rough day from start to finish, I was extremely exhausted. I laid in the hospital bed and fell into a deep sleep. I remembered vaguely that the nurses woke me up in the middle of the night to check my blood pressure and make sure everything was okay. The next time I woke up it was the next day. I looked around the small room. I heard nurses conversing with one another out in the hall. I gently touched my stomach. I couldn't believe I had had a baby—all by myself, with nobody there to hold my hand or tell me to push, nothing. I had to make some calls. I adjusted my pillow and sat up slowly in the bed. I leaned over and picked up the phone.

"Hello, is Jamal there?"

"No he's not." *Click.*

That bitch, I thought.

I dialed my mom's house.

"Naja?"

"Yeah?" my little sister asked, obviously upset that I had woke her up.

"Naja, guess what," I said, clearing my throat.

"What?"

"I had the baby," I told my sister proudly.

"Angel?"

"Yeah, who you thought it was?"

"I thought you was Mommy," my sister said.

"What, Mommy ain't home?"

"No."

"Where she at?"

"I don't know. Her and Marvin went somewhere last night."

"Where Kindle?"

"He at Aunt Jackie house. He spent the night. But anyway," Naja grew louder. "You said you had the baby?"

"Yeah, late last night."

"Oh, my God! Already? I thought you wasn't due 'til like July or August or somewhere around there."

"He was premature."

"Why?"

"I think it was because I been stressed lately. But they got him on these machines to help him breathe and stuff."

"Awww, I wanna come up there and see him. It's a boy?"

"Yeah."

"What you name 'im?"

"I didn't name 'im yet, but I'm goin' name him Curtis Jamal."

"Awww, baby Curt." Naja gave my son a nickname. "What hospital you at? I'm goin' come up there."

"MHC," I told her, "on First Avenue in the city."

"Oh, okay. Can you have visitors this early?" she asked.

"Yeah, I think so, but you can wait and come after school."

"Girl, please. I ain't goin' to school today. I just had a nephew. That's a off day for me."

"Well, when you come down here, bring Mommy with you."

"I don't know where that chick is," Naja said with an attitude.

"She shootin' up again?" I asked.

"Probably so, and I ain't chasing after no dope fiend. If I see 'er I'll tell 'er where you at and she can come see you on her own. I'm 'bout to get dressed and come down there now."

"Oh, and Naja, if you see Jamal, tell 'im I had the baby and tell 'im what hospital I'm in."

"He should be there with you. Where he at?"

"His mom trippin'. She ain't givin' him my calls."

"You want me to go next door and whip on her ass for you?"

I chuckled. "No. Just tell Jamal what I told you to tell 'im if you see 'im."

"All right."

"Bye."

I anticipated my sister coming up there to see me. In the meantime, I called the last person on my list, Elaine.

"I had a boy," I sang as soon as I heard Elaine say hello.

"Oh, my goodness!" Elaine shouted in the phone. "Congratulations!"

"Thank you."

"So, is he all right? It's kind of early isn't it?"

"Yeah. I was only five and a half months. He's okay. They got him in ICU. He still has a lot of developing to go."

"Yeah, yeah. Well, when did you have him?" Elaine asked.

"Last night."

"Um, March 26. I'm going to have to play three twenty-six," Elaine thought aloud. "So, what hospital are you in?"

"MHC . . ."

I was going to give Elaine the address, but she cut me off. "In Manhattan?" she asked. "On First Avenue?"

"Yeah."

"Oh, my goodness, that's where I had Brandon at."

"For real?"

"Yeah, child. I know exactly where you are. I'm goin' call the baby-sitter and see if she can watch the kids when they get out of school. If she do, I'm goin' come see you and the little man."

"Aww, that would be nice."

"What did you name 'im?"

"Curtis Jamal, after my brother and my boyfriend," I explained.

"Aww, that is so cute. Well listen, let me call Veronica now and see if she can watch the kids. If so, I'll see you later."

"Okay, Elaine."

"All right."

"Bye." I hung up the phone. At least I could expect two visitors that day, even though they weren't the two most important people—my mom and Jamal. When I got off the phone, I called for the nurse so that I could see my baby. I hadn't seen him since I glanced at him after they took him out of me. The nurse took me up to the intensive care unit. She walked me into the room where my son was. He was in an incubator with plugs attached to his tiny body. I got an eerie feeling when I looked at him, like he wasn't mine. I didn't know if it was because of how sick he looked or if it was the postpartum depression the nurse had briefly told me about on the way up. I couldn't explain the feeling I got, I just knew that it wasn't the feeling I expected to get the first time I looked at my baby. I thought I was going to feel love for my baby. But I didn't. Truthfully, I felt sadness. I didn't want him.

The nurse must have been able to tell that I was uncomfortable because she voluntarily started rubbing my back.

"It's difficult to see them like this at first, I know. But it's not as bad as it looks. Over time he'll grow and develop and start looking like a normal, healthy baby." She felt the need to offer an explanation.

But I wasn't sure if that was what was bothering me. There was something else. I just couldn't put my finger on it. I told the nurse that I was finished. She escorted me back down to my room and I crawled up in the bed and cried myself to sleep.

I woke back up around nine o'clock when they brought breakfast through. I felt a little better, but I didn't have much of an appetite, so I picked over the French toast. I did eat the little container of frosted flakes they gave me, though. I was drinking my milk out of the pint-size carton, and in walked Naja, looking like she was twenty-five instead of thirteen.

"You look all grown," I teased.

"And you look all fat," she teased back as she reached over to hug me.

"Why you got your cleavage all out?" I asked her, unable to help seeing her boobs popping out of the low-cut tanktop she had on.

"Don't be hatin'," Naja said, playfully holding her jean jacket together to cover her breasts. "So, where my nephew at? I wanna see 'im. Who he look like? I hope he got our hair and not Jamal's. I don't mean to talk about ya boyfriend, but he got some nappy hair."

"Shut up," I whined. "Talk when you get a boyfriend."

"Oh, I gots me a shorty," Naja bragged. "And he got that wavy stuff."

"You better slow down, miss. A shorty with wavy stuff will get you another shorty with wavy stuff," I told her with a look to match my attitude.

"Anyway, where is the baby?" Naja asked, excited.

I pushed the button to call the nurse. She came in the room.

"What do you need?" she asked, chipper.

"Can I take my sister up to see the baby?"

"Oh, sure. Are you up to it, though?"

"Umm, I think so, yeah," I gave her a half-ass answer.

"You sure?"

"Yeah," I gave a more definite response. I really wasn't

ready to see him again, but Naja had come up there for that purpose, so I didn't want to be like no.

I put on the footies and the robe they gave me, and Naja and me followed the nurse out to the elevator.

"You know what floor, right?" the nurse asked.

"Yes."

"Okay. You can go on up."

Naja and I took the elevator up to the intensive care unit. We walked down the hall, checked in at the nurse's station, and went into the room where my baby was.

Naja immediately put her hand over her mouth.

"Aww," she said as tears gathered in her eyes. "He is so tiny," she whined. "And pale," she added. She examined him, and I kept quiet because I still felt uneasy.

Naja walked around the incubator to get a look at his face, and then she frowned and blurted out, "He look like Marvin!"

That's what it was, I thought. That's what was making me feel so wrong about my baby. He did resemble Marvin. I got a flashback of Marvin on top of me, and I almost passed out. I grabbed my chest and stumbled. I backed away from the incubator and left the room.

"Angel, where you goin'?" Naja called out.

I ignored her. I ran down the hallway and pressed the button for the elevator. Naja was coming behind me but got stopped by a nurse who I guessed was asking her what was going on. I got on the elevator and pressed my floor number. Without thinking clearly I went into my room and took off the hospital robe and footies. I put on the jeans I had came there with, put on my sneakers, grabbed my coat, and walked out the room. I didn't think about Naja or the nurse or anyone stopping me. My mind was on one thing and one thing only.

Outside the hospital, I got in a cab. I told him where to take me and he pulled off. I put my face in my hands and cried uncontrollably on and off the whole ride. When the cab reached my mom's house I told him to wait there and I would come back out and pay him, but I guessed he felt sorry for me because he told me not to worry about it. I got out the cab and walked up on my mom's porch. The front door was wide open. "Make It Last Forever" was playing on the radio. I walked in the house, and my mom was sitting on the couch smoking a cigarette and bopping her head to the music. Marvin was stretched out with his head in my mom's lap. His eyes were closed, but he wasn't asleep because he was moving to the music, too. They looked like a small part of the *Good Times* painting that a lot of black people had in their homes. They seemed so happy and so in love. They were at peace. For a moment I wanted to leave them that way, but my mind was moving quicker than my heart, and I reacted with the same speed.

"YOU FUCKIN' BASTARD!" I yelled, abruptly spoiling my mom and Marvin's mood.

"ANGEL!" my mom snapped out of her trance and yelled back at me. "What the fuck is your problem?"

"What the hell's the matter with you?" Marvin jumped up.

I slammed my mom's door. My heart was beating over-time. I charged at Marvin, plunging at him with my closed fists.

"ANGEL! STOP!" my mom shouted as she struggled to grab me and pull me off of Marvin.

"You fuckin' drug-addict bitch! You gave me a baby! You raped me and raped me and gave me a fuckin' baby! You low-life! Fuckin' dope shooter!" I screamed every name in the book at Marvin while my mom held me back.

"What the fuck are you talkin' about?" Marvin asked angrily. He got off the couch and walked toward me and my mom. He had a look in his eyes like he wanted to grab me by my neck and throw me somewhere. His teeth were grinding and he was upset. But I didn't care. I wasn't scared of him no more. It was nothing left for him to do to me. When he got close enough, I spit in his face. That did it. He gripped me by my hair, forcing my mom to let me go. He grabbed my face and held it in his hands and squeezed so hard it felt like the blood circulation in my head had stopped. I thought my mom was going to pull him off of me like she had pulled me off of him, but all she did was stand off to the side, screaming.

"Y'all stop it! Marvin! Let her go! One of y'all is gonna get hurt! Please stop!"

Marvin let my face go. I stumbled backward.

"You better get your daughter, Carmina!" Marvin demanded.

"Angel, what is wrong with you?" my mom cried, obviously trying to make sense out of the whole ordeal.

"Mom, I just had my baby. A premature baby with plugs and tubes all over him," I sobbed.

"Well, we ain't got nothin' to do with you having ya baby early! Maybe it was that fuckin' weed you smoke!" Marvin yelled.

"I know, Angel. What are you talkin' about?"

"Shut the fuck up, Marvin! You shouldn't be sayin' shit! Fuckin' bum!"

"You got one more fuckin' time, Angel!" Marvin threatened.

"Angel, what are you startin' with Marvin for?" my mom asked.

" 'Cause he's the fuckin' dad! You don't fuckin' get it? He raped me, Mom! And he got me pregnant!"

"You told me that was Jamal's baby! Now you come in here and say that it's Marvin's. You ain't right, Angel! Why you goin' bring this shit here? Huh? What is it? The fact that we clean? You don't wanna see us happy, do you? Shit, Angel! I'm comin' up on five months, and you come in here with this bullshit!" my mom screamed.

I wiped my tears with my hand. "What? You think I don't wanna see you happy? Mom, all I been trying to do was make you happy. But no matter how hard I tried, you never seemed to get it. And now you think I'm comin' in here tellin' you that I just had your boyfriend's baby 'cause I don't wanna see you happy? Mom, Mom, Mom. You just don't know," I sobbed. "You don't know what ya little girl been goin' through. Mom,

I been to hell and back over these last two years dealing with you shootin' that fuckin' dope! And then when you brought Marvin in our house, a strange man you met in the streets, and you brought him around your daughters. You didn't think twice, did you?"

"Make her shut up, Carmina, or else get her out of here!" Marvin cut me off.

"YOU SHUT UP!" I screamed.

"I'm leavin'! I'm not dealin' with this shit!" Marvin said as he headed out the door.

"Marvin, wait." My mom tried to stop him. "Let me just get to the bottom of this!"

He brushed past my mom and kept goin' out the door.

My mom turned to me. Still crying she asked, "Angel, why did you do this to me?"

"What do you mean, why did I do this to you? You let that man in this house. You let him around us! I ain't do shit! He raped me!" I screamed almost at the top of my lungs.

"Then why did you come back?" my mom retorted.

The tears began to pour and so did I. "Mommy, I just had a baby! And I left him at the hospital because I couldn't stand to look at him. He looks just like Marvin. And for some reason you're mad at me for it! You know what, Antione was probably tellin' the truth. You probably did set Curtis up!"

"Okay, stop right there!" my mom yelled, seemingly holding back tears.

"No! Antione told me what you did! How you owed niggas and got Curtis killed tryna pay 'em back! And now I guess I'm payin' niggas back for you, too, huh? You owe Marvin some money? Was he ya bookie or somethin'? Is that why you let him rape me?"

Smack! My mom slapped me across my face and then fell to her knees. She started crying like I had never heard her cry before. I didn't care though. She was lucky I didn't slap her back. She was a pathetic bitch, and I was finally seeing that. She didn't deserve the title of Mom. All she did was use her kids. It was no wonder Naja disrespected her the way she did. She saw something that me nor Curtis saw. And that's probably why she'll be the one to make it, because she ain't fooled by that bitch balled up on the floor. My only hope is that she doesn't leave Kindle behind, when it all is said and done, because I can't do it anymore. I'm done.

"Mom, you think that slap hurt me? Please, you've done worse shit to me." I chuckled. "I'm out."

I walked out my mom's house and up the street. My heart was torn to pieces and my mind wasn't functioning properly. I felt like I was outside of myself. I was walking like a zombie, staggering and aimless.

Like déjà vu, the guy who lived in the crack house was sitting on his porch.

"Yo, you all right?" he asked.

I shook my head no and asked him if he had some weed.

"No, but I got somethin' better," he told me.

I walked up on the porch and he led me in his house.

It was kind of dark inside for it to be so sunny outside. All the shades were down. There were people everywhere. A guy and a girl were on the couch. They both looked asleep. Another guy was on the loveseat with an open can of Budweiser in his hand. There was a lady sitting on the floor with her head pressed against the wall. It looked like she was asleep, too, but she wasn't—because she was mumbling to herself.

"You stay upset about somethin'," the guy said leading me to the dining room. "But that's all right. I got somethin' that'll fix all ya problems."

We walked through the curtain that separated the living room from the dining room, and even more people were in there. But they all were awake, gettin' blasted. A lady and a man were sitting at the table sharing a crack pipe. A guy across from them was shootin' up. Different types of drugs and paraphernalia were placed in front of each of them as if they were place settings. The smell in the air was strong. I figured it was the crack, since that was the only thing being smoked. I couldn't compare it to anything, but it was a smell I would never forget.

"Sit down," the guy who had brought me in the house told me as he kept on into the kitchen.

I sat in the last empty chair in the dining room.

"Angel?" the lady next to me said.

I turned to her, and it was the lady who was in the Chinese store talkin' about she used to baby-sit me and my brother. I didn't know whether to speak or not. I mean, she was in there smoking a pipe and I was in there waiting to smoke something.

"Hi."

"What you doin' in here?" she asked while her companion sucked on the glass. "You smoke, now?"

"Weed," I replied.

She shook her head. "Ain't no weed jumpin' off in here."

"He got somethin' for me," I told her, tears forming in my eyes.

"What's wronnng?" she sang, looking me in my eyes.

I couldn't answer her. Images of my baby were running through my mind. I just started to cry.

"Aww, Angel, what's the matter? You know what, Squat takin' too long," she said as she retrieved the pipe from the guy she was with. "Here," she said, handing it to me. "Smoke it like you smoke weed. But don't take long puffs. Take short ones. Like this," she instructed as she hit the pipe.

I took it out of her hands to try it. I put it up to my mouth the way I saw her do it and sucked. The guy, whose name I found out was Squat, walked out the kitchen.

"Damn, you couldn't wait? I had some zanies for you. You don't need crack if you used to smokin' weed. You need something to put you down not get you up. Crack goin' have you goin'."

"You was taking too long, Squat. Shit. Plus she needed more than some damn pills. And this is my family. I used to change her diapers. I'ma look out for her," the lady told Squat.

"Well, that's on y'all," he said and left the dining room.

I sucked on the pipe some more, and slowly I started to feel in control. My senses seemed to heighten. I was more coherent and my mind started to clear. I was feeling refreshed.

Motherly Love

finished up the lady and the guy's pipe, and the lady copped us another bag. She said she had just got her income tax check so she was treatin'. The pipe was in rotation and I was about to get my turn when I heard my mom's voice in the living room.

"Squat, gimme a nickel of juice."

"This ain't enough."

"This is all I got until I get my money in two weeks."

"Well come back then, Carmina. You always do this shit."

"*Carmina?*" the lady I was smokin' with shouted. She must have been listening in like I was.

"Squat, give 'er what she asked for, it's on me!" she yelled.

I passed her back the pipe even though I didn't want to.

The fact of the matter was I still had respect for my mom. I didn't want her to see me smokin' crack. I didn't want her to see me in that house.

"What's wrong?" she asked. "Why you ain't hit it?"

I shook my head and wrinkled my face. "My mom comin'."

"Oh, please, girl. That's that crack that got you paranoid already. Ya mom is cool as shit. I grew up with ya motha. I know," she said, putting the pipe back in front of me.

After a few moments my mom walked through the curtain. Her eyes went to the other people in there first. And before they got to me, the lady stood up and grabbed my mom in a bear hug.

"*Carmina!* What's up, girl?"

My mom stepped back to see who she was. "Ne-Ne?" my mom had a slight smile on her face.

"Yeah! I got ya daughter over here!"

"My daughter?" my mom asked with attitude.

My mom looked past Nina, and her eyes landed on me.

"Angel! What the fuck is you doin'?" I never seen my mom look at me the way she did that day.

"Don't worry, I took care of her," Nina told my mom.

My mom wasn't trying to hear that. She threw a fit.

"Ne-Ne, that is my daughter! You don't take care of her like this! She is a child! She don't need to be in here!"

Nina sucked her teeth, "Carmina, it's me! Come on now. Ease up. We used to do our thing back in the day, too. What, you forgot?"

"You are not understanding me, Ne-Ne. That is my child you got over there," my mom said, as she glanced over at me and then onto the table in front of me. "And she smokin' crack?!" My mom flipped out. She immediately started to cry. "Angel, what the fuck? Do you know what you doin'? Baby, you are gonna fuck ya whole life up!" Then she turned to Nina. "Ne-Ne, you really crossed the line. I ain't seen you in over ten years and you bring my daughter in a crack house and introduce her to this shit! You used to watch her. She was like ya child. Would you have ya child up in here smokin' a fuckin' pipe?"

Nina's happy attitude turned mad. "My child do smoke crack," she said, pointing to the guy she was with. "So what you sayin'? Just like you shoot dope and ya daughter smoke crack! It's a cycle, Carmina! What you expect?"

"Ne-Ne, you got five seconds, Ne-Ne. I swear to God I will fuckin' jam this loaded needle in ya neck! You better get the fuck out my face right now! I swear you got five fuckin' seconds."

Nina started gathering her stuff. "You like my sister, Carmina, and I got a lot of love for you. That's the only reason I'm leavin' without kickin' ya ass. Come on, Tee," she said, leaving with her son.

"And you!" my mom walked over to me. She shook her head. "I guess I did this, right?"

"Mommy, not right now, okay. Just go 'head and shoot up and let me be," I finally spoke. Just because she showed some concern for me didn't mean anything. I was still mad at her.

All the stuff she had done up until that point outweighed that one time she acted like she cared.

"Let you be? For what? So you can smoke the rest of that pipe?"

"Mom," I whined. "It's not the time. It's really not," I brushed her off. She was right, though. I did want to get back to the pipe. It was calling me. But somehow I still had enough respect for my mom not to pick it up and smoke it right there in front of her.

My mom sat down in the chair next to mine and put her hands on my knees. "Angel, listen. I know I haven't been there for you these last two years, and I may have caused all this. But you don't have any idea how that situation with your brother affected me."

"I do now," I snapped. "Now that I know that you had something to do with it!"

My mom started shaking her head. "No, no, no. It was not like that at all. All I did was tell the guys where he would be. They was not supposed to shoot my son. You hear me? They was not supposed to shoot my firstborn!" My mom's tears came plunging out her eyes like water from a busted pipe. "I fucked up with Curtis. I'm not sayin' I didn't. But I don't want to fuck up with you."

I butted in, "Well, it's too late 'cause you already did."

"I know. I know. But none of that other stuff you did made me realize how bad I fucked up with you like seeing that fuckin' crack pipe in front of you. When you was makin' money however you was makin' it, runnin' away from home, gettin' locked up, gettin' pregnant, none of that opened my eyes. That was just the way shit went as far as I was concerned. But, Angel, I can't tell you how I feel seeing that crack pipe in front of you." My mom broke down.

I looked away from my mom, uninterested. I wasn't in the mood for all the mushy shit. When I needed her a few minutes ago it was all about Marvin. Now she wanted to tell me how she felt and all that. Well, she was too late.

"What can I do to convince you to get up and leave that pipe?" my mom asked, still holding on to my knees.

"Mom, why are you buggin' out? You came in here to get high, didn't you? Talkin' about you clean. Clean, my ass."

"Angel, I *was* clean. I was doing good, too, even when Marvin came back, I was doin' good."

"No, you wasn't. Don't even lie. Naja told me y'all stayed out all night."

"When? Last night? Nooo. We wasn't out gettin' high. I took Marvin down to the detox center, and my friend was on duty. She let me stay there with him for support, that's all. That's why when you came in earlier, we was both so happy. And it caught me off guard, when you started talkin' like that. 'Cause I felt like we had finally beat our demons, and we had planned to start all over. And then . . ."

"Well, I didn't know that!" I finally unleashed my tears.

"Of course you didn't. And I didn't know that Marvin had hurt you! I was so messed up all the time. My mind was never in the right place. I was either high or thinking about gettin' high. I can't remember one time that my mind was on anything else. And I'm so sorry. But I know now, and I want to be your mother and do what a mother is supposed to do. I want to get you out of here and I wanna get you some help," my mom cried.

I shook my head no. "You didn't come in here lookin' for me. You came in here to stick that needle in ya arm."

"I know. I did. After you told me about your baby and then you brought up Curtis, I couldn't take it. I was gonna use my last three dollars on a hit and say fuck it. But, look what happened. God intervened, Angel. God brought us together, mother and daughter, both with our fuckin' addictions, and he wants us to stop together."

"No." I shook my head. "You say all that now like I'm supposed to just forget about all the stuff I been through because of you. Like I'm supposed to just take ya hand and walk out of here with you like everything is peaches and cream."

"I don't expect that. I know I messed things up for you. I know it's goin' take time to fix it all, but just give it a try. I'm tellin' you, you don't want to keep up no addiction. You don't wanna be no fuckin' crack-head. Ya whole life will be wasted. And I'm speaking from experience, Angel. Two years of my life just passed me by like that. And I know the rest of it will do the same thing if I keep shootin' dope. And if you start a crack habit now, at only fifteen, you know what the next twenty, thirty years is goin' be like? Hell. Pure hell."

"That's goin' be whether I smoke crack or not, living with you," I told my mom spitefully.

My mom gave me a look. I must have hit a nerve. She picked up the needle that she had put on the table when she first sat down and looked like she was going to put it in her arm.

And since she had the audacity to shoot up in front of me, I was going to smoke in front of her. I picked up the pipe and put it in my mouth. Then I felt a sharp pain shoot across my chest. The pipe dropped from my lips and onto the table. I went to clutch my heart and my mom's hand was in the way. I fell over somewhat and my mom caught me in her arms. She pulled the needle out my chest and cradled me. She started rocking me back and forth and sobbing over me. My vision got blurry to the point that I could hardly see. I felt my body shaking, and I was going in and out of consciousness. I heard echoes of somebody screaming. Then I felt my eyes roll to the back of my head and I saw blackness. My body stopped shaking and the screams turned to silence.

I thought my mom was about to get high when she picked up that needle. I thought she was going to let me smoke the rest of the crack. I thought we were going to get high together like Nina and her son. She was so desperate and so hurt, I just knew she was going to shoot her dope and not care about me being there. She could have easily given up and said to hell with you, Angel, go ahead and spend ya life in turmoil. But she didn't. She finally stepped up to the plate and protected me as a mother should. She stopped me from spending my life as a crack-head and used her last three dollars to do it. Now, you might think that's nothing, but having done drugs before myself, I know that must have been hard. She wanted that dope so bad. It was in her eyes. But she used her last hit on me and put me out of my misery. I guessed she figured she had given me enough of hell and maybe it was time for her to give me heaven. Now, that was love. She finally showed some motherly love.

We come from troubled wombs.
Our homes resemble tombs.
We come from polluted souls.
Our lives resemble holes;
empty and devalued, longing for the close.

While you're taught monsters don't exist,
we're feeding from their breasts
forced to carry the weight of their fate upon our
malnourished chests.

Our role models are zombies
whom we refer to as our mommies
in love with vampires that suck the lives out of
their bodies.

We live amongst the dead
who walk around with empty heads,
numbing their brains just to feel sane,
revealing skeletal remains.

We come from troubled wombs.
Our homes resemble tombs.
We come from polluted souls.
Our lives resemble holes;
empty and devalued, longing for the close.

Acknowledgments

Thank you Allah for allowing me to get this one written. It gave me a hard way to go at times, but it was worth the struggle.

Rich and Amir, you two already know what it is. My sincerest thank yous go to you both.

To my family and dear friends, thanks for all you do. The part you all play in my success is exceptional.

And to everybody who had a hand in getting this book to the masses—Liza Dawson, Simon & Schuster, Cherise Davis, Martha Schwartz, Dawn Michelle, distributors, retailers, vendors, etc. along with everybody who picks it up, recommends it, or supports it in any way, thanks much and I appreciate you the most.

See you again in a few months.

Ya girl,

Miasha